CW01514701

The Arctic, the Inuit and the Polar Bear

Dave Hill

Copyright © 2016 by Dave Hill. 516251
Library of Congress Control Number: 2013915078
ISBN: Softcover   978-1-4836-8793-3
        Hardcover   978-1-4836-8794-0
        Ebook   978-1-4836-8795-7

All rights reserved. No part of this book may
be reproduced or transmitted in any form or by
any means, electronic or mechanical, including
photocopying, recording, or by any information
storage and retrieval system, without permission in
writing from the copyright owner.

Print information available on the last page.

Rev. date: 11/30/2015

To order additional copies of this book, contact:
Xlibris
0-800-056-3182
www.xlibrispublishing.co.uk
Orders@ Xlibrispublishing.co.uk

I have dedicated this book to Megan my wife, who I met at school, ever since then she has helped me to fulfill my dreams and I will love her until the day that I die.

And also to my Inuit family who looked after me for three weeks on the frozen sea whilst we were hunting. Andrew, Roland and Qamayuq.

To Adrian,
Best wishes

David
2 September 2024

It's only 21 March. It is just over a month until my birthday on 24 April, but Megan was already asking me how I would like to celebrate my sixtieth birthday. She was racking her brains out trying to find something different for me, that what I would like to do to celebrate this milestone in my life. A family gathering, a big party, go to a nice restaurant for a special meal, or maybe she could cook one of my favourite dishes, and we could knock down a couple of bottles of nice wine before I opened that special vintage malt whisky that I had been specially saving for this occasion. It would be as old as me, a rare bottle of Ardbeg from Islay an island off the west coast of Scotland. My grandfather, old Pop Lowes, had bought two bottles when I was born, one for my christening which I am told wiped my brow before they polished it off. The second bottle was for me to open whenever I wanted. I deferred it from my fiftieth birthday, but it was not going to be reprieved from blowing its top when I hit sixty. Ardbeg was his favourite tipple of the glens. It is revered around the world as the peatiest, smokiest most complex whisky of them all. Yet it does not flaunt the peat; rather the peat gives way to the malt and the natural flavour subtly intrudes on the palate producing the perfect balance. Ardbeg is a malt to which all the others aspire and has been so since 1815. I really enjoy my malt whiskies, but as yet had never tasted this special dram, although I had been tempted to open the bottle on more than one occasion and come April, I will not wait any longer. As you have probably guessed, I opted for a nice home-cooked meal and having the family around to enjoy it with me. To me it was just another notch on my stick, this time I would be sixty instead of fifty-nine, one year older.

All this changed after a chance conversation with Joe, my hunting agent in Montreal. I rang him to discuss the moose hunt that he was organising for me in the fall. He had reserved me a hunt in the Yukon/Northwest territory where there were plenty of moose. It is a wilderness left mainly to the native Indians and an area not frequented by too many white hunters. He said that I would be virtually guaranteed to shoot my trophy moose, as much as you can guarantee anything in hunting, but at least the opportunities should be there. Out of the last five moose hunts, I killed one young cow, and on the second, I shot a young bull, both in Newfoundland. The others were a total abortion and I had been ripped off. The guides in Newfoundland told me that if I wanted a good trophy, I would have to go west and north, which I was about to do for my next hunt. After we had finished discussing of the arrangements for the hunt in the Yukon, I asked Joe if there was anything else that I could hunt before September, half-knowing that the answer would be no before I even asked the question. 'Not really, most of the hunting starts in September.' Then he casually said, 'You could of course go on a hunt for a polar bear in the Arctic.' I nearly fell off my chair. 'Yeah, I am sure I can. I thought polar bears were a protected species and were on the endangered list with "CITES". You are just pulling my leg, Joe.'

'No, seriously, the Inuits are granted several licenses each year by the Canadian government. Some of them they use for themselves, but others sell to foreign hunters, for which they charge a lot of money.'

His remarks seemed so glib that I did not even bother to ask him how much it would cost as I never expected that there would even be an opportunity so late in the day. This brings in a lot of money into the community, and by God, they do need some extra financial support.

'What is the best time to go hunting, Joe?'

'April or May is probably the best. At that time of year, the bears have very good skins and are out on the sea ice hunting for their main source of food, the seals. Bears really need a lot of food. The females have to suckle their young who have just emerged from their winter dens, and the males need to get strong and fit and ready to mate and prepare for the next winter.'

'I am sixty on 24 April, and if you can manage to organise a hunt for me so that I am in the Arctic on my sixtieth birthday, then I will go.' I was so excited at the prospect of hunting with the Inuits that I did not even think of what else I should be doing or about my forthcoming birthday party which Megan was about to organise. At such late notice, I never thought that Joe would be able to pull it off as my birthday was only four weeks away, but if he did, then this would really be an extra special experience to remember for all the rest of my life. Hunting in the Arctic was never on my wish list and hunting for a polar bear had until now, never before even entered my head.

Well, that is how it happened, I never expected Joe to come back and say that he had managed to organise an Arctic adventure. Not only did he come back, he also said that he had managed to get it so I would be hunting on 24 April. This seemed like a dream. I was up there on cloud nine. Even while sitting at home and talking to Joe on the telephone, my adrenaline was running high. My heart was pumping so fast that it must have been up at least ten beats to the dozen, and I never stopped asking him questions for half an hour. The phone call lasted for well over an hour, and when we finished, I went to tell Megan the news, 'Darling, please do not worry about my birthday surprise, I am off hunting in the Arctic to hunt a polar bear.' Her first reaction was the same as mine, 'You can not kill a polar bear as they are protected'.

I said that I thought that too, but went on to explain the situation, 'Believe me or believe me not, I love nature, animals, and natural history and very passionate about all kinds of wildlife, but am also a selective and enthusiastic hunter and opportunity to hunt in the Arctic Circle for a polar bear was a chance in a lifetime not to be missed, and the opportunity only arose because the government in the United States had banned the importation of polar bear skins and their body parts. No American hunter was going to spend a fortune to hunt a polar bear and not be allowed to take it home. This opened a small window of opportunity until they found new hunters to take their place. Alas, the window is now closed and has been filled by very rich Russian businessmen to which the expense is no problem, and they will pay whatever it takes to secure the limited hunting permits!'

Megan was quite upset, as were my parents for me even considering to hunt a polar bear. They did not mind me hunting animals to eat but to hunt for a trophy and for my own ego and personal satisfaction, they found rather distasteful. When I told them we were going to eat it and that polar bears are a part of the Inuits' normal diet and had been so for hundreds of years, it watered down their objections just a little. Others only believe what they see on television and see them as the graceful giants of the Arctic and they hold them with the same esteem as they do the male lions in Africa. No one raised an eyebrow when I brought back a black bear from the states, so what is the difference? If you can kill a black bear or brown bear, what makes a white bear something precious? They have got the same life and deserve to live just as much as the polar bear does, and it is only because some people view it as the icon of the Arctic that it commands a higher level of respect.

The big white polar bear is something special. It is an endangered animal and is listed as species to be protected. However, this view is not strictly true. There are plenty of polar bears in the Arctic, and their demise will be caused by global warning which will permanently change their environment, so they will be unable to hunt and that will cause their extinction. Hunting alone has not and will not in the future be the last nail in their coffin; the blame is clearly and undisputedly caused by the whole of mankind who has until only recently ignored the irreparable consequences of how the modern world has been developed at the expense of future generations of all kinds of wildlife and of man himself. Inuits have hunted polar bears for hundreds of generations, and there was never a problem with polar bear numbers in Arctic until white man interfered that they had a perfect balance with nature.

I have had many discussions with lots of people on the merits and ethics of hunting and shooting and believe that I can justify, convince, and win a debate with anyone who eats meat. From my personal experience, I can give them a vivid description of animal cruelty and how lambs, cattle, pigs, and poultry are slaughtered and their lives from the time they are loaded onto a lorry at the farm, how they are subjected to continual and unbelievable stress when they are unloaded at an auction market, forced down gangways into pens, and mixed with other animals that they do not know and have never met before. They are chased around a sale ring in a noisy, unknown and to them a horrific environment with an odd beating with a stick for good luck, before, they are reloaded into a truck with no space to move and worse than sardines in a tin (but remember unlike the sardines, they are still hopefully alive). They then can be driven, for over twenty-four hours and in some cases longer in these conditions, before they reach the point of slaughter at an abattoir where they are eventually dispatched, in away which some people still believe is humane. On arrival at the abattoir, they are first put in the lairage which is always adjacent to the killing lines where they can hear the frantic calls of other lambs or pigs as they are hustled into the stunning pen. The rampant smell of fresh blood is everywhere, and they may be subject to having to stay in this environment for several hours before it is their turn to die. The stress that we cause to our animals so that we can eat meat is unbelievable, and if the ordinary man in the street knew exactly how they were treated, I think it would stop many of them ever eating meat again. If it did not, then I am quite prepared to fill them in with even more gruesome details, which I have purposely omitted as I did not want to deliberately upset my readers.

I actually shot two roe deer this morning. They were both grazing in the open field about 100 yards from the edge of a wood. It was midmorning, and the winter sun was on their backs. They were keen on filling their stomachs and only occasionally looked up. Meanwhile, I went well around them and then crept through the wood towards them. I quickly checked their sex, both were does, and in season so I shot the first doe which dropped instantaneously; for one second, it was eating away with not a care in the world, and the next second, it was dead. The second doe looked up on hearing the shot. It had not the slightest notion what caused the noise or of my whereabouts and then continued grazing, until it too was humanely dispatched. Neither of these deer underwent any stress whatsoever. They were both dead before either of them heard the shot (except the second deer heard the shot when I killed its friend).

I believe that people should focus their minds on the cruelty and suffering of humans on other humans before they start worrying about animals. That is not to say that you ignore what is happening in the animal world, but they need to have completed some basic research before criticising hunting carte blanche. After all, we all need to eat; man has been hunting for food since the days of the caveman, and when domestication came, breeding animals for human consumption was a new conception. Most people when they buy a sausage, steak, or chicken breast are not concerned about how it got to the supermarket. They do not link the sausage to the pig rooting away in the orchard or the steak to young bullock quietly grazing in the meadow filled with grasses, herbs, and flowers or even the chicken which is scratching on the midden looking for grubs. As a seasoned traveller who has had the good fortune to have been able to travel to many parts of the world and with my strong interest in agriculture and especially animal production, I have seen cruel practices which would be totally abhorrent and appalling and would immediately raise your hackles and make the hair on your arms stand on end, even the most voracious human carnivores would immediately turn into a vegan or be a vegetarian if they knew how cruelly we treat our animals before it is served on a plate, which has no resemblance or association to the animal we are eating. You have by now probably gathered that this subject is dear to my heart and one of my hang-ups. It is not that I am trying to make a case out for hunting, but it is a genuine feeling and that I care about animal welfare. I feel that man could drastically reduce the stress that he causes to farm animals in the way they are reared and slaughtered. The birds and animals which we eat are not immune to our actions. They can also feel pain and have highly developed senses, and they do have a brain which allows them to feel mental as well as physical stress. Even if you do not have any sympathy for the livestock, there is a massive wealth of research proving that preslaughter stress causes a massive reduction in meat quality and it is in our own interest to improve animal handling, transport, and slaughter welfare.

When I was sixteen, my aunt arranged a vacation job for me, at Cavaghan and Grays; they were bacon curriers on the outskirts of Carlisle where she worked. This was my first insight into the food processing industry and how we treat and slaughtered our pigs. My grandparents used to rear pigs, and the pigs that they reared also went there for slaughter. Moo's pigs were happy pigs, (Moo was my grandmother. I gave her this name when I was toddler and ever since then everybody has called her Moo until the day she died) . They were well-looked after and were very clean animals, which is not the general perception that most people have of pigs. When I was a little boy, they were my pets, and she often found me fast asleep amongst them in their cosy bed of straw. They kept their bed very clean and did their business outside in the yard. Pigs are instinctively very clean animals. You do not have dirty pigs, but you do have dirty masters who rear them in overcrowded and dirty conditions. Our way of rearing pigs was very much the exception rather than the rule, as most pigs were raised in 'factory farming' conditions; the term itself indicates a pressure environment, and I had first-hand experience of this, as when I was at university studying agriculture, one of the topics was the problem of tail biting in pigs. Some producers used to cut the tails off at birth so that they had nothing to bite. They then started biting the ears of other pigs. What were they going to do then, cut off their ears? I raised this point only to illustrate the cruel conditions that some farmers used to rear their animals, in ways that the meat-eating general public never know about. In my early days as a toddler, I spent much of my time at my grandparents' farm. This was a very exciting, informative, and conditioning time in my life and was the beginning of my future love of animals and nature and the highlight of my holidays as a young boy.

The first sign of man's cruelty was when the lorry came to pick up our pigs and take them off to Cavaghan and Grays for slaughter. We walked them quietly up from the pig sties to the loading bay. The lorry driver had a slap marker which worked like a tattoo. He would slap very hard on both the hams and shoulders. This was the first time that our pigs had felt any pain. These tattoo marks would be on the pigs forever and could even be seen on the hams and bacon when they were displayed in the shops.

The real cruelty started when they were unloaded at the lairage which was next to the slaughterhouse. Do not run away with the idea that pigs have no brains or fears. The pens were next to the killing pens, and while the pigs waited their turn to be dispatched, they could hear her brothers and sisters squealing and snorkelling and they could smell the blood coming from the slaughter house. The stunner had a pair of electric tongs which when placed over the pigs' head delivered a mammoth electric shock which stunned them. The pigs fell to the floor immediately, and another guy put a shackle around one of their legs which lifted them up to the bleeding wall where the slaughter man slit their throats and the blood flowed into the channel below. If this was not bad enough, some pigs were not properly stunned, and I've seen them hanging by one leg, jumping up and down on the shackle, until they broke free and dropped fifteen feet, landing in a trough of blood. Covered with blood and scrambling to get out, the pig was beaten with a steel bar to try to stun it so they could take it back to the killing pen. The stunners and bleeders show no mercy, and these men have no feeling for the animals that are in its distressed state of mind. (I hope you are still able to enjoy your bacon or joint of pork.) I can relate many other slaughter experiences with cattle, sheep, and poultry in both the UK and abroad but rest assured they are not pleasant and I'm sure that I do not need to continue this theme any further. Realistically, the farmer and the others involved in meat production cannot totally remove stress from animals which have to be killed. The meat that you enjoy on your table is the final product made from those baby chicks, piglets, little lambs, and calves that you see jumping around in the fields or hidden away in the factory farms. I am now pleased to see that as a result of the efforts of many animal rights lobbyists that things are slowly changing and you the final consumers are now willing to pay more for their meat, milk, and egg in order to stop the production from factory farming systems and have their food produced in an animal friendly environment.

In my opinion, the average hunter kills his quarry with less stress than either lions, tigers, or many other predators who firstly carefully stalk their prey and when close enough give chase. Even here there is more stress to the prey than me hunting them, and in many cases, the animal has a very slow death and is ripped apart while it is still alive. This cruelty from animal to animal is something that will never change; however, there is no escaping from the fact that I am a predator too and on occasions I do not kill an animal outright and therefore it will suffer, but it is very rare that I miss an animal on the first shot. I am not trying to justify why I hunt as I will never convince anybody who is against blood sports or a vegetarian that my actions are either necessary but they are humane, especially if I am not a purely trophy hunter and hunt for food, I feel that I can justify my actions. However, I firmly believe the death of the animals I shoot is more humane and less stressful than the way our domesticated animals are reared and slaughtered. There is one particular example when I do give an animal a less stressful death that it would have otherwise have. On my farm and on many other farms, the fox is a very real problem, especially at lambing time as it will kill baby lambs for pleasure as well as for food.

There are three possible scenarios: firstly, I could shoot it; secondly, I could ask the huntsman of the local foxhounds to come onto the farm with their foxhounds and hunt. They would find the fox and then proceed to rip it apart; or lastly and most unrealistically, I could take the view of some people who thinks that the fox has a right to live even if it is feeding its cubs with my lambs. I am not going to allow the last suggestion; otherwise if you take that argument to its logical conclusion, I would go out of business or stop keeping sheep. So if I was Mr Fox, I would either keep off my farm or opt for the bullet; it is an easier way to die than me bringing in the hounds.

I feel that I have justified my right or decision to hunt and now I am looking forward to my journey to the Arctic and the challenge of living and hunting with the Inuits. March soon passed into April, and before I knew it, I was sitting in Edinburgh airport waiting for a plane to Montréal via Amsterdam. When I'm travelling long distances, I like flying with KLM. Their business-class service is excellent, and when you get to your final destination, you are not tired and feel quite refreshed.

Joe was already in Arctic Bay, and I was to be met at the airport by Louise, his wife. She was a French-Canadian and was going to be my host for two days after which she would drive me to Ottawa to catch a plane to Arctic Bay. She had everything organised for me; firstly, she would take me to my hotel which is in the middle of town so that I could rest and have a shower, and then she would pick me up at 8 p.m. to go out for the meal. Louise is a very chatty lady and had first-hand experience of Arctic conditions. She started to get me very excited and caused my adrenaline to rise when she was describing the hunt that I would be taking in the Arctic. Joe had rang her from Arctic Bay to check if everything was going according to plan and that I had arrived safely. He was looking after two Russian hunters. They had flown there in on their own private jet and Joe had to stay with them as interpreter and he would be waiting for me when I arrived in Arctic Bay. He had left instructions for me with Louise. There was a long list of the clothing and equipment that I had to buy in Montréal which I would have had difficulty in buying in Scotland and Joe had said that it was cheaper in Canada.

It took a good half-hour to get from the airport to the Sharon Hotel. As soon as she pulled up, the genitors were waiting to uplift my luggage. Louise came in with me to the hotel reception desk to check me in. I was greeted with a smiling face and a cocktail which was the signature drink of the hotel.

Everything was well-organised. All they needed to do was to swipe my credit card. I then finished my drink very slowly as it was an excellent cocktail and not to be rushed, all that I had to do was to take the elevator to the fifteenth floor. It really was a very pleasant room, and they had left flowers, chocolates, and snacks on the dresser. The mini bar was filled, and for a change and to my surprise, they were all complementary.

Louise said that she would pick me up in two and a half hours, so I had plenty of time to relax and have a bath. It really was a luxurious suite with a big corner spa bath and even a television in the bathroom. They had left a nice bottle of white wine on ice next to the bath. I was not going to drink it at first as I did not want to spoil my dinner, but what the hell, so I decided to open it. It was an excellent way to start my Canadian adventure, and I knew that my accommodation in the Arctic was going to become more frugal, so now was the time to enjoy the luxury, have a drink and a chocolate, and then retire to the bathroom for a long, hot spa. I lay there surrounded by bubbles, watching a game of American football, and sipping my wine. It was so warm and cosy, and the vibration of the bubbles sent me to sleep. I was not awoken by the telephone, but the persistent knocking on my room door by one of the staff eventually alerted me and asked me to answer the telephone. I didn't even need to get out the bath to answer it, and when I did so, the receptionist said, 'Mr Hill, there is Miss Louise waiting for you in the lobby.' I told her that I'd be down there in five or six minutes. I quickly jumped out of the bath and started to dry myself. Although I had been sleeping soundly, I really felt refreshed. I took a clean shirt out of the suitcase, and within minutes, I was in the elevator and was soon down to meet Louise. 'Hi, Dave, how was your room? Do you feel adequately revived after your long journey, and are you ready to hit the town?'

'The room is great. Thanks, Louise, and the bath has really livened me up.'

'What kind of food do you like?'

'I like nearly anything except tripe which I've tried in lots of different recipes but just can't get my head around it and eat it. Other than that I'm pretty easy to please.'

'Fish or meat, Dave?'

'Oh, let's go for the fish.'

'That's a good choice, Dave. We really have a very, very good fish restaurant downtown. Come on, we will have to go. I've left the car just outside the hotel and Bellman won't be pleased if we leave it there any longer.' We jumped into the car and were off. The fish restaurant was in the south end of town, but the evening rush hour was over, so it did not take us very long to find it.

We were busy chatting away when all of a sudden Louise hit the brakes and there was a large screech. A motorcyclist had just come through the red lights and only missed us by inches. 'Well, that's a good start to your Canadian adventure. Let's hope you get home in one piece.' The restaurant was called Le Homard, and even at this early hour, we struggled to find a place for the car. It was only eight o'clock and restaurant was already over half-full. The car park was at the rear of the restaurant, and you had to go through their fish shop when you entered the restaurant from it. There was a spectacular array of fish some of which I did not know despite the fact that I'm fairly well up on recognising different species of fish. I love scuba-diving and fishing and have read as many books on diving and fishing as they are in the local library. You could see by their gills that the fish were very fresh, and in addition to this, there was two large tanks holding crayfish, lobsters, and many kinds of crabs.

The head waiter greeted us and tried to show us to a vacant table in the middle of the room. 'Is this okay for you, sir?'

'Not really,' I replied. 'I prefer to sit at that table in the corner of the room.'

'No problem, sir.' He took our coats and then returned with the menus for us to peruse. I have quite a hang-up about where I sit in a restaurant. I like to look out with my back to the wall. When I go out with Megan, she knows exactly where I will or will not sit, and when a waiter pulls out a chair for her to sit on, she has occasionally has had to tell him, 'Oh no, that chair is for my husband.'

'Would you like cocktail to begin?'

I was about to say 'no, thank you' when Louise quickly said, 'Yes, that would be very nice' and asked for a brandy briquette. I had not a clue what that was, but she said, 'Try it, Dave. It really is a nice drink.' It really was a very pleasant cocktail, and now I know how it got its name; there are three frozen cubes of a brandy liqueur floating in a mixture of Grand Mariner, vodka, and home-made lemonade.

The menu was basically all fish, but there was also a few meat recipes; however, most of the guests had had come especially for the fish. Firstly, you had to go back into the fish market which we passed through as we entered the restaurant. They had a fantastic display of teens of fish, from very many parts of the world and a good selection of fresh local fish. Fish of the day was halibut which had just been flown in from Alaska, as were the crayfish and spider crabs. You really were spoiled for choice. They all looked so good that I was never going to decide, so I asked the fishmonger to guide me and recommend a fish. He suggested the monkfish with lobster and an oyster sauce. It did not sound bad to me, so that's what I plumped for. Louise ordered the halibut which is one of my favourite fish, but I decided to stick with the monkfish. We both had a spider crab soufflé which turned out to be totally out of this world. She asked me to choose the wine, so I opted for a Canadian Chardonnay from the West Coast. The dinner was a gastronomic delight and fit for any table. We both completed the meal with the same sweet as I followed Louis's lead and ordered the chocolate roulade with wild berries and a vanilla sauce. This like the hotel was a tremendous start to my adventure.

We weren't in any hurry and did not leave the restaurant until 10.30 after which Louise returned me safely to my hotel. 'I am busy in the morning, but I'll pick you up sharp one, is that okay, Dave?' I thought for a second or so and then said that 'I'm sure that I'll find something to do until then. I'll go for a wander around the shops. I can spend hours browsing around.' I then thanked her very much for the meal and bid her good night.

I decided to stop at reception and asked them for the price of my room and I was a bit taken aback when they said it was $350 and breakfast is served in the lower restaurant at a cost of $45 each. I had guessed that it was probably fairly expensive but not that much. I was meant to be there for two more nights but decided to check out the next morning. I am not mean but I have a far better way to use my money and so long as I find somewhere that is clean and respectable, I don't want to be paying $350 per night. I only hope that I don't embarrass Louise by telling her so. I checked out the next morning and asked them if I could leave my suitcase there until I'm collected by Louise at one o'clock. This was not a problem to them so that was what I decided to do.

While I was browsing through the hotel literature before I hit the sack and I noticed that there was an exhibition for the work of John and Yoko on the opposite side of the street and only 500 yards away from the hotel, so I decided to have a look in at their work first. I have always loved John Lennon as an artist and a songwriter and two of his songs are in my favourite top ten of any songs and in fact are at numbers one and two; these are 'Imagine' and 'Woman.' To my surprise, there was no entrance charge to the exhibition which had

travelled all over the world and was a total insight into Lennon's personal life. I would have gladly paid twenty pounds as an entrance fee and I'm sure many of the people there would also have paid that. (See I'm not really mean.) The hours passed very, very quickly, and before I knew it, it was time to return to the hotel to meet Louise. One of the exhibits that was there was John Lennon's white piano, the same one which he used to write the song 'Imagine'. Some of

the visitors were sitting on his piano stool and having their photographs taken, so I decided to ask someone to take mine as well, which would be a very nice keepsake. It would make Lennon even more precious and rememberable, which would make me feel even closer to him and his work. I quickly walked back to the hotel to find Louise already there and waiting for me.

'What's the plan now, Louise?'

'We've got to go to shops to buy your Arctic clothing, sleeping bag, and anything else that you might need.' I told her my feelings about the hotel and that I felt it was a big waste of money and hoped that I did not offend her, but I had checked out and wanted to stay at a more reasonably priced hotel. Luckily, Louise is a pretty easy-going girl and was not upset at all. She said that Joe automatically booked all of his hunting clients, most of whom were very rich Americans who only wanted to stay in the top hotels. As I had never discussed this with him, he aired on the side of caution and booked me into one of the top quality hotel in the city. Now that Louise knew what I wanted, she would find me a nice respectable hotel, the Holiday Inn or something similar. We set off to the stores which sold suitable clothing and would keep me warm in the Arctic. The basic philosophy about keeping warm in such cold conditions, which do change slightly from day to day, is to build your body clothing up in layers so if you are cold, you put on an extra layer, and if you're warm, you remove one. There is a massive choice of clothing. You can have full body suits or tops and separate bottoms and also different thicknesses of materials with different 'u' values. We were recommended to take one full bodysuit and four tops and four bottoms. One of the brands I purchased was called 'thininsulate', and it was so thin that I wondered how it would even keep me warm. We went through the same procedures for socks after which we had to choose the boots, which were designed specifically for Arctic conditions and would keep your feet warm down to minus forty, but we had to find them in another store. Then we had to move to yet another shop to buy my sleeping bag. This again was guaranteed to keep me warm down to minus forty degrees centigrade. The last thing we needed was a large waterproof bag to take all my equipment and clothing. Once we had bought this, we would have finished shopping.

Louise then took me on a brief tour of Montréal. One of the places we visited was Chinatown. I have been to many Chinatowns that are in many cities in the world, but I never get bored with visiting another one, as they are so different in culture and sell merchandise which we can't get anywhere else. We decided we would like some fruits to eat, so I went into a Chinatown greengrocer to buy some pears as they looked and smelled delicious. One of the other fruits which I noticed were on special offer was kumquats. They were very good value and do not ask me why but I bought 3 kg of them. I wasn't to know then but they proved a useful supplement when I was in the Arctic.

It was now 6.30 going on seven, so Louise said it is time that we went somewhere to eat. 'I'm going to take you to a pub which brews its own beer on the premises and braai's excellent steaks. I remember that you said that you had a passion for real ales and I'll introduce you to a good friend and business colleague of Joe. He's a great guy and I think that you will like him.' The design of the pub was spectacular, and it looked as though it was the film set of a bar in an old Western movie. Louise knew exactly where she was going and made a 'B' line for a table where Dmitri was already waiting for us. Dmitri was Russian and has been a friend of Joe for a long time. He had lived in Montréal for eight years and spoke very good English but now has moved back to Russia. He sends many clients to Joe, and in return Joe sends some of his clients to Russia and many other places where Dmitri organises hunts. As soon as we sat down, a waiter pounced on us and brought us the menu. I've been in these home-brew pubs in America and Canada before and they all serve a taster tray where you get eight or ten different beers to sample and this one was no different to the others except each shot was a quarter of a pint and there were twelve beers to sample on each tray. I could see that there were some serious beer drinkers. The starter tray was three pints and that was just to wet your appetite. I started with this so that I could choose which beer I preferred to have with my meal. Dmitri and Louise both drink beer and they knew exactly which one they wanted. They suggested that I go for a T-Bone. You get a really good steak here, and I must admit the Americans and Canadians know how to produce good beef, and what's more important is they know how to hang it and barbecue it to perfection. America and South Africa are two of the countries that I have never had to send a steak back to the kitchen because it's tough and overcooked. I love my meat rare or even blue and have done so since I was very young. My folks don't eat it unless it is well done and as tough as old boots. I remember going out to dinner with one of dad's colleges. He ordered a rare steak and when he cut into it, you could see that it was well done. He called back the waiter to complain, 'I asked for a rare steak.'

'Sorry, sir, I do apologise.'

'Well, go back and tell the chef that I want the steak kiss the pan and not to fuck it.'. I'll never forget my parents' faces when they heard those instructions, but it was Denis that started me eating rare meat.'

Louis and Dmitri both went for surf and turf with a twelve-ounce New York strip

topped with lobster tail, side salad with ranch dressing onion rings and chunky fries. They knew what they were doing and exactly what to order and so that I didn't get the feeling that I was missing out. They told the waiter to throw in a lobster tail onto my T-bone. The meal was scrumptious and excellent steak cooked to perfection, nicely charred on the outside and rare within. The only downside to the meal was they didn't have a decent mustard. Their yellow mustard is great on a hot dog, but that's about all it's good for. After ploughing through my beers with the help of some nibbles, I opted for the wheat beer to drink along with my meal, and as you can imagine, it was a hell of a feast, but there was not a scrap left on any of our plates and we didn't need a doggy bag as I had seen some people leaving the pub with. We did not leave until well after one, and both Louis and Dmitri were well over the limit and ordered a taxi to take us home. Louise was going to be picking me up from the hotel at eight in the morning. She suggested that I take the spare room at her place as it would save a lot of time and trouble tonight and later on in the morning. She does not normally do that kind of thing for their clients, but I was already not one of their normal clients. She felt very relaxed about it and I could only take it as a complement.

Dmitri was back in Canada to meet some new clients arriving in Montréal the next day and then take them up to the Arctic to hunt but not to Arctic Bay. He as well Joe really does mollycoddle their clients. They are both at the premium end of the hunting fraternity and it is the quality of their service, the attention to the small details, choosing and using the very best outfitters who have a proven track record of successful hunts, which allows them to charge high fees to hunting clients, who are always satisfied with the hunts they organise, even at times when they do not get the trophy they desire. During the meal, I was quizzing him about what he offers. He can virtually fix any type of hunt and for any quarry but specialises in South American hunting for a panther, in Asia for the Marco Polo sheep and of course in Arctic hunts for polar bears and walrus. I told him that I would be interested in hunting for a Marco Polo ram, the sheep which is the pinnacle for sheep hunters. He told me that when I was ready, he would organise a hunt in Kazakhstan on the steppes near the Chinese border and as a contact of Joe, he would give me a very good deal. We closed the meal with a double Jack Daniels on ice, after which we parted company. He would only have a few hours sleep as his Russian clients were arriving at some unsociable hour the next morning.

We went back to Louise's place. She showed me to my room, and I was dead to the wind within minutes and still sound asleep when Louise woke me the next morning. I felt very guilty because she had already taken a cab to pick up her car and had prepared the breakfast of pancakes with streaky bacon, tomato sausages, and maple syrup followed by chocolate muffins and Italian coffee, which is just as popular in Canada as it is in the UK. I said that after last night's extravaganza, I was not really hungry, but she told me to tuck in now when I could, as she could not guarantee what I was going to be given in the Arctic and I might need to use every calorie that I have in my body to survive out there. I knew that she was labouring the point, but after all the effort that she had made, it would have been very rude of me not to accept her hospitality and eat her excellent breakfast.

After breakfast, I packed the Arctic clothing and the rest of my luggage into my new waterproof bag including the kumquats and a kilo of whole almonds and some hand warmers which Louis gave me, and then left everything else that I did not need into my suitcase which I was leaving with Louis.

We then packed everything into her car and set off for Ottawa airport to catch my plane to Iqaluit which was my first stop on my journey to Arctic Bay. I was all booked in, had gone through passport control, and waiting at gate eleven when the tanoy announced there was a delay to my flight as the plane had not yet left Iqaluit; it was bound to be at least a four-hour delay, and we were being offered meal vouchers to sustain us while we waited for our plane to arrive.

In years gone by, the white man had claimed all the Inuits' land when they colonised Canada, lands where for generations they had lived peacefully in equilibrium with nature as semi-nomadic transvestite race of people. In winter, they lived on the ice. The open sea was frozen for months, and they hunted polar bears, seals, and walrus for food, to make clothing and tents, and to use the bones to make weapons and carvings, like many other aboriginal people all over the world. They built their homes close to the source of the animals which they hunted. When their quarry moved on, they abandoned their houses and built new ones. This was easy to do as their shelters were made from frozen snow of which there was an inexhaustible supply. These houses which we call iglus could be constructed in less than a couple of hours from start to finish. The frozen ice floors were covered in different animal skins which were a good source of insulation, and they had a fire fuelled by oil from the seal blubber. Inuits lived in small family groups which were scattered all over the frozen sea but kept in touch with each other using their sledges as transport. There is no timber in the Arctic, and they were both versatile and dextrous and had learned the skills of lashing which they used to construct their sledges. In those days, they used every material available to hand to build their sledges, all of which came from animals. They used Arctic charr wrapped in seal skins and lashed with sinuses to make the runners and the rib bones of whales for the transoms, and with this type of construction, the sledges were very flexible, and as the sinuses got wet, they tightened and held everything in place.

They domesticated the wild dogs and used them as animals of burden and also to pull the sledges using skin from the bearded seal to make the harnesses. Out there on the ice, they had to be totally self-sufficient to survive and to use every trick in the book which they passed down from each generation. The family groups were closely knit together, but when different families met, they would exchange food and clothing.

As the sea ice melted from the open sea towards the land, they made their retreat and spent the summer months on the land hunting caribou, gathering berries, fungi, and herbs, and drying them to add flavour to their winter diets.

During the summer, their homes were usually tents made from animal skins or some homes were made from earth sods which like the iglus could be left behind as they followed the herds of caribou. Their other main occupation during the summer months was to fish, mainly for Arctic charr which they would preserve by salting and drying or by appropriate freezing.

Using skins, bones, and sinuses, they made sea-going vessels called kayaks to fish from and then they worked in tandem with other families to hunt for narwhal. This is a member of the whale family, and it is one of the delicacies which the Inuits really relish and enjoy. It has a skin which makes good leather and grows a very unusual tooth that can grow in a spear-like form to well over six feet long and is good for carving and making tools, particularly spears.

This closely woven and interactive bond with nature has sustained Inuits' life for teens of generations, and it is only in the very recent past that the influence of so-called modern man has completely and irreversibly forced changes in their lifestyle which many Inuits regret. Inuits are proud of their heritage, and as a people who were dispossessed of their homelands by the new white men who colonised Canada, it took until 1982 when Canada's Constitution Act recognised the Inuit as Aboriginal people in Canada. That their rights and part of their homelands were restored to them as being the legal owners and allowed them to develop as a distinct nation once again with their own homeland.

The first contact with the new Canadian immigrants was probably with the Hudson Bay Trading Company which made the initial changes to Inuits' culture and lifestyle. Previously, they were totally self-sufficient, but the Hudson Bay Company introduced new materials like wood, steel, and the introduction of guns, snares, and traps, enabling them to make their sledges with timber, have iron tools, nails, and receptacles.

From Ottawa, I flew on to Arctic Bay via Nanisivik. We were grounded because of the weather and had to have an unexpected overnight stay in the most basic of basic hotels. The weather was so bad that the airline could not guarantee that we would fly in the morning, and I had to contact Joe to let him know that I would not be arriving that day.

It took until lunchtime for the weather to improve enough to let us fly, and I began to wonder just how bad the weather would be when I was out on the ice with my Inuit guides. They would be used to these horrific weather conditions, but I had never ever been subjected or experienced to a temperature less than minus five degrees centigrade and that's without any blizzards or snowstorms which may hit us.

As we were approaching the runway, I got my first view of Arctic Bay which was bigger than I had expected. Joe and my guide were waiting to meet me. This was the first time that I had met Joe, although we had spoken on the telephone for several long conversations, but when we met, Joe seemed quite nervous. He had planned and was hoping to accompany me on the hunt and apologised that he was not there to greet me on my arrival in Montreal. He had to change plans as his elderly father was ill, and he had to make some last minute changes because two Russian hunters had changed their plans and he had to accompany them, but he had nothing to worry about as Louise was an excellent host.

He introduced my guide as Andrew who was small-built man and had very dark complexion and greeted me with a very wide smile. He was wearing a red cosset-type hat, the significance of which I would find out later. Although it was just a short journey of twenty minutes from the airport to Arctic Bay Village, even twenty minutes was too much too long. I've seen better vehicles in one of those stock car races or even in a scrapyard. I don't think Andrew's car was good enough to even go into one of those races; however, we did eventually get to the village. Andrew's Dodge pickup had one rear door missing and hinges on the front door had been welded on. The inside was nearly completely gutted except for the two front seats. Even they were not the originals, while the rear seats comprised two upturned beer crates with no cushion on top and you're right, they were not very comfortable.

Two miles from the airport, Andrew stopped the truck and pointed out Arctic Bay. From this elevated position, you could see that it was a small but long village, and it was nestled next to a mountain range which gave it some protection from the harsh westerly snowstorms which were frequent and continued for most of the winter.

There appeared to be miles of flat land off to the east of the village which again was encircled by mountains but was in fact frozen sea, the whole Arctic Bay was frozen solid throughout the winter. As we approached the village, you could see lines of dogs chained to the ice which covered the sea. This is where they spent every day when they were not used for pulling sledges. Only a few had any shelters, the rest were subject to whatever storms were thrown at them and lay there curled up, lying only on their feet at minus forty degrees below. God knows what our animal lovers at home would have thought; probably they would have rung the RSPCA.

Andrew drove us to the village which was an unplanned ad hoc mixture of houses with a shanty town appearance. We approached what was the village hotel, and it did not look an inviting place to stay. It was a long tin building painted grey, and it looked to be unoccupied and semi-derelict. Oh my God, what have I let myself in for now! Well, at least I am only here for one night and then out on the ice with Andrew. I will just have to make do with this flee pit, which on first appearances seemed to be worse than any place in Africa that I have had the misfortune to inhabit and I have stayed in some dives when I've been there. To my surprise, Andrew drove past the hotel, and three junctions later, he turned to the right. Immediately in front of us was a spectacular newly built building with a twenty-first-century design, and it had a brilliant location with views over the bay and towards the mountains. Joe had sat in the back with the dogs and could not wait to get out and I think his arse was really aching.

Once inside the guesthouse, he introduced me to Clare the proprietor who was waiting with a fresh brewed coffee and home-made muffins. The interior of the house was immaculate and extremely luxurious. I've stayed in hotels all of the world and this small guesthouse was miles ahead of anywhere I had previously stayed including some five star hotels. It was a dream house and its tranquillity and ambience blew you over. I have never seen a building with such an atmosphere which is hard to describe other than to say that it made you feel like a king in his palace.

After coffee, Andrew left us saying that he had to make the final preparations for the next day and would pick us up at six in the morning as he wanted to get off to a quick start. We had over two days to travel to the hunting area and I was bubbling with excitement at the prospect of living with the Inuits. I could not wait to go and explore the village and make my initial discoveries of how the Inuits live. This was my first experience of living at thirty below and I was told it would get even colder. Firstly, I had to go to my bedroom and unpack my Arctic clothes which I bought in Montréal with Louise. Joe said it is absolutely essential to wear this exterior clothing as it takes time for my body to adjust to the temperature.

Outside, the scenery looks inspiring, a cloudless blue sky with endless white snow covering many of the roofs of the houses. It looked like a Christmas scene out of a fairy tale. It was so inviting to step outside. I really was still sceptical about the necessity of wearing the Arctic clothing and could not believe that it was so cold. I hate wearing hats and gloves, and at home, I never ever wear gloves and only wear a hat when I go stalking as it prevents scaring the deer with my white-grey hair. It did not take a couple of minutes before my hands felt icy cold, and I was forced to quickly put on my gloves. It might not be obvious that it is thirty below, but it made me suddenly realise that although you can't see the cold, you can feel the cold temperature immediately you expose yourself to it and that might be just too late. Oh hell, what will happen when I wanna piss? Will my willy get frostbite and drop off? As Joe and I set off on a brief wander around the village, we saw the sign the tourist information centre and made straight for it. God knows why they wanted to provide a tourist information centre. Where were the tourists? There was no one on the plane with me and I only think it can be hunters that will come to Arctic Bay. We had only been wandering around for twenty minutes and already our faces felt really cold, and it was a relief to enter the tourist information office. I was very pleasantly surprised as I just expected a little pokey corner somewhere with a few leaflets; however, there were two members of staff, leaflets, and maps everywhere, not just of Arctic Bay but also other places in the locality, and there were lovely craft displays of carvings from both wood and stone, paintings, and Inuits' clothing which was all made out of fur and leather from seals, caribou, and polar bears. I was particularly fascinated with the carvings especially those from stone. Their intricate detail highlighted the skills of the local carvers. I glanced at the prices, and believe me, they weren't cheap. I suppose they have so few tourists that they have to make their money from the ones that do come out to Arctic Bay. Probably there may be more tourists in the summer when they can visit the other national parks in the area.

There was only ten minutes left before they closed, so I quickly had a good look at the local crafts and grabbed some brochures of Arctic Bay and the hinterland. We then headed back to the hotel passing two churches, the village school, and the shop on the way back. The shop was very sparsely filled with goods, but it sold everything from a tiny screw to an iPad, a slice of whale meat or polar bear mince to a full frozen dinner something like we can buy at home. They did stock some of the Western brand names like Coca-Cola, Cadbury's chocolate, and even believe it or not, HP sauce. They also had fresh vegetables which had to be imported on a regular basis, and this reflected heavily in the prices. One green pepper cost over three pounds and a bunch of bananas topped £10. I wondered how they got the money to pay these extortionate prices for the things that we take for granted and are so very cheap to buy in Scotland.

It took us quite a few minutes to head back to the hotel which was only a few hundred yards away and was within our view because the roads were so icy and you had to watch otherwise you could have a bad fall and have a serious injury and would have to miss the hunt. The heat hit us as we entered the door and removed our snowy boots and clothing. Clare could hear us enter and yelled out, 'Dinner will be ready in ten minutes, so if you want a wash, get one quickly as I don't want dinner to spoil.'

'What are we having?'

'You'll see when you come down,' he wasn't giving any secrets away. Joe and I quickly went upstairs, had a wash, and got changed ready for dinner.

The table was now set for four which puzzled me as I knew that Clare had had his dinner with his family and I haven't seen anybody else in the hotel, but when we came down, a lady and gentleman were already seated at the dining room table. They both stood up to introduce themselves as John and Jenna. John was in the village for two months to train a new teacher and update another. The village school had thirty-eight pupils between four and eighteen years of age. After that anyone who graduated from school and required further education had to leave Arctic Bay to go to a university. Jenna was a researcher and was monitoring mixed-age classes as one teacher had a class with children ranging in age from five to fourteen. This really stretches the teacher's ability and also causes them a lot of stress teaching such a wide age group in the same class.

We all then sat down to eat. Clare would not tell us what the first course was, we had to guess. It was some kind of smoked meat with a side salad and had a slight fishy taste. It tasted delicious, but no one guessed exactly what it was. Clare was in the kitchen quietly listening to our deliberations, and when he came to collect our plates, he put us out of our misery and told us that it was smoked seal. The next course was equally delicious, but we all managed to guess what that was. It was Arctic charr served with a wild fungi sauce. I didn't know at the time but Arctic charr was going to be one of the main ingredients of my diet when I was out on the ice hunting with Andrew.

After dinner, Joe asked Clare if he would call Peter and asked him to bring along some of his carvings for us to look at and hopefully buy. He lived only a few houses away and suggested it would be better if we go to his house as we could see the range of his stone carvings. Most of them are animals, but he had a few that were abstracts showing Inuits' culture and heritage. The one that struck my eye was a carving in marble of an Inuit hunter harpooning a narwhale. Joe also liked this carving and said that if I did not want to buy it, then he definitely would. Although it was a fantastic piece of art, I really was looking for a carving of a polar bear which would remind me forever of my trip to the Arctic. The narwhale is a spectacular animal. One of its teeth has grown into an ivory tusk which can often reach ten feet of solid ivory. Peter's carving also had a tusk which was carved out of a piece of ivory. I asked him how much he wanted for the carving and was rather shocked when he told me the price. Joe quickly said that a good deal, you would have to pay five or six thousand dollars for it in a gallery in

Ottawa. Although it wasn't what I wanted, it was so good that I decided to buy it. However, deep in my heart, I still really wanted a carving of a polar bear. When I said this to Peter, he said that if I wanted a polar bear, he would carve one specially for me. I asked him how much he would charge, and he said he would do it at the same price as the narwhale. I started to haggle and tried to negotiate a little bit about the price, but he was very firm and insisted that the price was a fair price and wasn't going to give me any discount on it. I then said that I would pay him the price he asked but he had to do a little carving to each of my grandchildren and teach me the basics of carving when I returned from the hunt. 'How many grandchildren have you?' 'I've got four.'

'So you want four carvings.'

'Yes, one for each grandchild.'

'Okay, that's a deal.' And we shook hands on it.

'What posture do you want your polar bear to be in?' I knew exactly what I was looking for as I had seen plenty of pictures of polar bears in books, magazines, and on the television. As it was a private commission, he would carve it exactly as I described it to him. 'I wanted the polar bear standing on its back legs, leaning forward, and ready to pounce and catch a baby seal under the ice.'

'No problem, I'll have it ready when you come back.' I was very lucky to find Peter as he was one of the best stone carvers around. The sheer thought of having a artisan who I have personally met to carve a polar bear exactly as I would like to see it in the wild was inspiring and got me very excited. My only worry was that I was not putting the cart before the horse and did not put a jinx on my hunt.

I asked him how long it would take him to carve the polar bear and could not believe that he could carve it so quickly. He was making very good money. If I could carve like him, I'd make a fortune. Although it was still expensive, you can understand why he needs money as the cost of living there was four or five times that it was in the South. The South is a term they use for anyone in Canada who lives outside the Arctic Circle. Anyway, stuck out in Arctic Bay, he would not get many customers to buy his carvings, and galleries in Ottawa would charge for five times the price they paid him for all his skill and hard work. I really felt pleased that I could give something back to the intuit community.

After chatting for another half hour so, Joe and I returned back to Clare's place for hot chocolate before retiring to bed. When we got back to the house, John and Jenna were still up and were talking to Clare. We had intended to go straight to bed, but we sat down and joined in the conversation and eventually retired to bed some hours later. We learned a lot more about Arctic Bay and the Inuits and also found out how and why Clare, a southerner, had settled in the village. He was originally posted there as an officer of The Royal Canadian Mounted Police and met Marisia who was an Inuit lady, born and bred in Arctic Bay. They fell in love and got married and the rest is history or so they say.

It took me ages to go to sleep. I couldn't stop thinking about getting out onto the ice and hunting for a polar bear. The whole idea of actually being there was beyond my wildest dreams and was an experience which I would appreciate more and more and will forever be engraved in my mind. Arctic Bay was little village nestled beneath some tall mountains and the sea. With people choosing to live in extreme temperatures and where you had twenty-four hours a day light for most of the year and twenty-four hours of darkness for the remainder, it made you really wonder why they had chosen to live in such a hostile climate.

My sleep that night was very spasmodic. I kept wakening and checking the time on my watch, but the hours seemed to pass very slowly. Everything had happened so quickly since my initial conversations with Joe, and now I was here, miles from home and waiting for morning to come. This was proving very difficult as it was light outside. I knew that if I did not get any sleep, then I would be very tired when I had to spend sixteen or eighteen hours travelling on a sledge. I desperately tried to sleep and eventually covered my eyes with one of those eye covers that I was given on the plane, put on my earphones, and listened to some music. This helped for a couple of hours, but I was so restless that I decided to read the literature that I collected from the tourist information office.

I was first down to breakfast at five o'clock, and Clare was already in the kitchen preparing breakfast. 'Would you like a coffee, Dave? I've got one going on the stove. Just help yourself.' It was the first time that I had been alone with Clare and started to quiz him about his life in Arctic Bay. He was obviously not a native of Arctic Bay but had now lived there for fifteen years. As I said he had been an officer in the Royal Canadian mounted police and married a local girl and decided to make their full-time home there. He had actually built his home himself and had made an excellent job of it, but all the materials had to be imported from the South, and it was not cheap to build such a spectacular home in Arctic Bay.

Breakfast was traditionally Canadian, smoked streaky bacon fried to a frizzle laid on a home-made pancake and smothered in Maple syrup and topped with a runny poached egg. I don't normally have a big breakfast, but this would be the last home-made meal I would have for three weeks, so I stuck into it and even had seconds.

We had just finished breakfast and Andrew arrived to greet us. 'You're not ready. You have to hurry up and get dressed in your Arctic gear as we've got to set off soon. We have a long way to go today.' I returned to my bedroom to put on my Arctic clothing, and I started the journey with five layers of clothing. Next to my skin was a very thin fully armed vest which was guaranteed to keep me warm at very low temperatures. The next one was of similar material but probably twice the thickness. Next I wore hand-knitted polo jumper made from alpaca wool. This in itself was very warm and I used to wear it in Scotland quite a bit in cold weather. Down below, I wore two layers of thinsulate long johns, followed by my trousers. I then put on my ski suite and finally put on my Arctic trousers and jacket which was the first line of defence against temperatures which may go down to below fourty degrees centigrade. Once dressed, I picked up my travel bag. It was large and fully waterproof and contained all my spare clothing, my binoculars, and two bags of goodies to help keep off the hunger and give me energy to keep me warm. I brought along a bag of cereal bars of various flavours and even included some Kendal Mint cake which was a very dense high-energy tablet, and most of the Arctic and Antarctic explorers used to take it on their adventures. This is sold all over the world and made in Kendal, a town in the Lake District where I used to live. Lastly, I had 1 kg of almonds which Louise had bought for me in Ottawa and the 3 kg bag of kumquats which I had bought from a Chinese grocery store also in Ottawa.

The bag was very heavy, and I struggled down the stairs trying to avoid scratching the decor. Joe saw that I was in difficulties and came across to help me carry the bag and put it in the truck. Andrew suggested that Joe should climb in the back again as he had done when we came from the airport, but Joe declined his offer and decided to walk from the hotel to the sledges which were parked on the sea of ice at the far end of the village. It took Andrew and I only a few minutes' drive to reach the sledges. It was difficult to see which was land and which was sea, but when he drove right next to the sledge, I knew we were definitely over all the water.

As I started to get out of the door, his son was across to help me to collect my luggage and tie it onto his sleigh. He introduced himself as Roland . The expedition involved three snowmobiles each pulling a very large sledge. Andrew's sledge was designed to carry the dogs. It had rectangular sides about two and a half feet high. The compartment had horizontal bars at intervals of two or so feet, to which the dogs were tied. Roland's snowmobile was pulling my sledge on which Andrew had made a little cabin for me to sit in and protect me from the elements. The seat in the back of it also had an upturned plastic beer box as a seat but this time Andrew had provided a cushion for comfort. He had cut out a window in the front so I could see what was going on and screwed on some clear perspex to protect me from the wind. The tents, skins for the floor, and some of the provisions were tied down in front of my cabin, and there was 75-gallon drum of diesel behind me. The third snowmobile was driven by Andrew's close friend,Qamayuq and a member of the fish and wildlife committee. He was pulling one of the most important pieces of equipment which we would need when we got to the hunting area. This was the dog sleigh, a lightweight and smaller version of the big sledges which the dogs could pull even with two passengers and hopefully a polar bear. He also carried two large drums of diesel, and there was a large box in the front which contained the remainder of our provisions for the hunt. They took enough supplies to last for four weeks, in case any problems arose, and we all had to return on the dog sleigh.

All we were waiting for was for Andrew to load his dogs. They were tied down by a long chain which was anchored to the ice at both ends. The dogs were tied far enough apart along the length of the chain to prevent them from fighting. These weren't the well-known furry husky dogs which are associated with the Arctic and the frozen north which you see on the Canadian tourist advertisements with the Royal Canadian Mounted Police. These were hungry ,mean working dogs who obeyed every instruction from Andrew. As he approached the line to untie the first dog which he wanted to put in sledge, an unbelievable crying and howling chorus echoed around the amphitheatre of the frozen sea. They knew what was to happen next, and they were going to let everyone else know that they knew what was about to happen. The noise was a cross between a yelp, a bark, and squeal and varied in tone from a soprano to a deep base. No sooner was it untied from the chain that it nearly knocked Andrew clean off his feet as the dog raced to reach the sledge where it was tied to one of the bars on the sledge. Andrew then returned for the second dog, and it too went through the same formalities screeching at the top of its voice and racing to the sledge. There were fourteen dogs in all, and it took a good quarter of an hour to get them on board their sledge.

Once this task was completed, we were ready for off. I walked across to Joe to say goodbye as he was flying back to Ottawa the same day. He wished me luck, and I thanked him for arranging this hunt and then turned back towards the sledge where the team were waiting for me to climb on board and we set off for the hunting grounds. As I climbed on board, the crowds who had gathered around waved and shouted, 'Good luck! Good hunting!' I then climbed inside my cabin and sat down on the makeshift seat. I turned around and gave a last wave goodbye. We were off. Andrew shouted at the dogs that were yelping and told them to quit howling, and they immediately stopped to the last dog. He then started to pull away, we followed Andrews sledge and then Qamayuq came in behind and followed ours.

Once we were on the move, I started to relax. I was still extremely excited and filled with anticipation and a little apprehension about what was to come. This was when I noticed the first problem. Andrew had designed and built the cabin specially for me as he felt I needed extra protection from the weather, but he made one mistake, he had put the window opening too low. This would have been perfect for an Inuit hunter but was a problem to me. The Inuit people are not normally as tall as southerners and I had to bend and arch my back in order to look out of the window. This was okay for a while, but after an hour or so, my back really began to ache. I do suffer from a weak back in any case but the only way I could reduce the pain was to sit up and look at the woodwork above the window. This was exacerbated by the vibrations of the sledge. After a fresh fall of snow, the ice ahead and as far as you can see looked as flat as a pancake, but in reality, that was not the case. The frozen sea ice underneath the snow went up and down up, and down and up and down, and each time it bumped over a ridge of ice, the vibrations were amplified, as was the pain in my back. I then decided to try and sit on the floor, so I took the cushions off the crate and kneeled on them. This allowed me to look directly through the window and my knees were acting like a buffer by absorbing the shock waves before they could reach my back. This proved to be a far more comfortable way to travel, but it too had some problems as I got cramp and my knees began to ache as well. Andrew had made such an effort to make me the cabin that I did not like to tell him, so I decided to endure the pain. After about two hours, Andrew stopped, and we had a quick coffee and a walk to relax and relieve the aches and pains. I now knew that this trip was not going to be a simple pony ride. With two days of travelling on the sledge, this was going to be more of an endurance test.

After the break, Andrew headed due west. We left the frozen sea, and our journey took us into a deep valley. The mountains were white and iridescent with only an occasional rock ridge breaking through the frozen white snow. The scenery was stunning, and mountain peaks made a magnificent backdrop against the clear blue sky. As we progressed, the mountains closed in on us from both sides and we started to enter the canyon, known to the Inuits as the black rock gauge. It really looked spectacular, and where the ice overhung the rocks, there was display of thousands of icicles hanging like stalactites and sparkling in the sunlight. They looked so delicate and fragile. It was a spectacular sight). We headed up this canyon for further six hours to reach the top of the pass. This was an exhilarating experience and one that I would not have missed for the world.

Apart from two or three breaks to exercise and pump our blood through our bodies, we had now been travelling for over twelve hours from the start of our journey at Arctic Bay. I had filled my pocket with the almonds and kumquats that I had brought from Ottawa and had been nibbling away at them. The kumquats were even better than one of those 'Walls' fresh orange lollies which I adore when I'm at home, the fresh juice oozed out as I chewed the frozen fruit. Andrew stopped his snowmobile and walked across to us to see that I was okay, as he knew that I would be finding it difficult adapting to my new environment on my first few days on the ice. He said that he would like to keep going for another three or four hours and was just checking with me, as I was only one that was not moving very much and I had to keep exercising and moving within my cab, otherwise my circulation would definitely slow down. Since I moved from the crate onto my knees, my back was a lot more comfortable and told him that I was quite happy to keep going for a while.

It's very hard to describe this scenery as it is nothing like I have ever seen before; the peace, the tranquillity, and the purity of the endless white snow is unbelievable and electrifying. It is constantly changing and holds your attention all the time, and although the scenery is white mountains after white mountains and more white mountains, it's never boring and hours tick away quite speedily.

Andrew was very happy. We had completed the first phase of our journey without any problems and decided that we should make camp now. It's rather peculiar because if you are undertaking the journey for a day and decide to make camp in the evening when the light is fading, there is a beginning and an end to each day. We are  now in the land of the midnight sun with daylight for twenty-four hours each day, where you have no natural indicators of went to start and when to stop. In this Arctic wilderness, your day is decided by two factors: when you're hungry and when you're tired.

Now that we had stopped to make camp each man with the exception of myself knew exactly what they were about to do, while I stood there like as spare prick at a wedding, as an observer and watched. The first task that Andrew undertook was to lay out the chain, so he could tie his dogs up for a rest, allow them to stretch their legs and pay a call. It was a very long chain, of some hundred yards or so, and I helped him to pull it along the frozen ice. He anchored it into the ice at the end by digging a tunnel so they could pass the chain beneath it and anchor it down. It surprised me how strong the ice was, but he used the same method time after time and it never failed. On the previous occasions when we had stopped, there was little or no reaction from the dogs. They were still lying down very patiently, but this time was different, they knew they were going to be released from the dog sleigh. What was to come was a repeat of their songs when they were going to be loaded into the sledge at the start of the journey. If you close your eyes, you may not have guessed who was singing; it was perfectly in tune and fully synchronised with the lead dog as conductor, and it could have been mistaken for an operatic recital.

Andrew walked back to the dog sleigh to untie the first dog which immediately jumped out and pulled him towards the chain where he tied it down. I was about to remove a second dog, but he shouted across telling me not to. He removes them in a specific order and ties them down on the same part of the chain where they had been previously tied. I left him to it and went to see if I could help Roland who had started removing the tents and other equipment from my sleigh. I asked him if I could help, but he insisted that I was the guest, and I was not there to do any work which was an uncomfortable feeling for me and went against the grain, as I was embarrassed getting this VIP service and would have loved to help. However, on this occasion, I did as I was told and stood watching exactly what they were doing so that I would be able to help next time. By the time that Andrew had tied all the dogs down for the 'night', Roland had erected the tent and was now starting to put down the ground sheets. Firstly, he laid a big piece of polythene over the ice. This was then covered in corrugated cardboard followed by seal skins with the hair-side down to the ice. It was then topped with caribou skins, this time with the hair upwards. By laying it this way, he increased insulation capacity which allowed us to keep warm, while we slept.

We did of course all have highly insulated sleeping bags which are guaranteed to keep us warm at below minus forty. While Roland had erected our tent, Qamayuq had been putting up a small tent for himself and now joined us in our tent where Roland was starting to prepare our meal. He had a small set of the rings fuelled by pressurised gas (petrol to us). This was not only used to cook the meal but also used to keep us warm. As the hunting guest, my meal was prepared first. I waited in anticipation to see what he would serve me out on the ice and miles from habitation, what was going to be my taste of Inuits' food, and much to my surprise and total disappointment, he had cooked me a pork chop, frozen peas, and sweet corn (which sounds silly as everything is frozen) with reconstituted potato. This was the first food that we'd had for eleven hours as when we were travelling, we just had a nibble of home-made bread and raw Arctic charr. Roland then started to cook their meal. He emptied the contents of a large plastic container into the pan and started to reheat it. I didn't know what it was, but it had a pleasant smell and looked very appetising.

I asked Roland what they were eating, and he told me it was caribou stew. I asked him if I could try it. He passed me some in a bowl to taste. It was very nice and I would have preferred to have it instead of the pork chop. 'Why did you not give me caribou?'

'I gave you white man's food, Dave, because all our previous hunters would not eat our food. They prefer to eat their own type of food.'

I asked him not to give me any more white man's food. I explained to them that I had come there to live with them and would like to eat their food. He looked very shocked and by their reactions Andrew and Qamayuq were too. There was some stew left in the pan and I asked Roland if I could have that to eat. He said, 'No problem, I'll swap your dinners. I don't get pork chops very often as they are so expensive.' I thoroughly enjoyed the caribou. This meal set the pattern for the rest of the hunt. From now on, I was going to be eating like an Inuit.

The next day I asked Roland what we were having for dinner and he said that we were having seal stew, I said that sounds great, he was astounded with a vacant expression on his face. 'What did you say, Dave?'

'I asked to make plenty of seal stew for me .'

'You want seal stew?' He still looked very surprised and said, 'We have never, I mean never ever had a hunter who wanted to eat our food.'

'Well, you have now. I did not come here to eat white man's food. I want to eat what you eat and do what you do.'

'That's great! We are both happy now.'

I really enjoyed the seal. It was a lot better than the seal that I tasted in Newfoundland. I was pleased that my dietary requirements had been sorted out, as it would have been a missed opportunity if I had eaten white man's food for the whole of the hunt. We were now starting to get ready for bed. This was about to be my first experience of sleeping in the Arctic at minus forty-degree centigrade, and my worry was as to whether my sleeping bag would keep me warm. When I got inside it, I did not think that it was very thick. It did not seem very thick at all, but Joe had assured me that the materials used were the state of the ark insulation and was one of the by-products discovered in the space technology, which now had uses outside the Apollo space programme, no more duck or goose down, they were no good for these extreme temperatures. The bag was zipped up right to my chin and the wrap around hood only left my nose exposed. I felt as warm as a bug in a rug and was so tired that I drifted into deep sleep within minutes.

The next morning, it took several strong shakes from Andrew to awaken me. It was home from home as he passed me a hot cup of coffee just like Megan does at home, except she serves tea. Breakfast is made whenever you are ready. It's pancakes and crispy bacon smothered with maple syrup. Oh what a delight! I never expected the Inuits to enjoy that, but they had really got hooked on it and had now become a regular dish for their breakfasts.

Andrew had already had his breakfast and went outside to start to tie his dogs into their cabin. I did not need to look out of the tent to see what he was doing because as usual they let out their spectacular chorus which was a nice accompaniment to my breakfast, after all you don't get a full live orchestral recital in every hotel. We quickly knocked off our pancakes, rolled up our sleeping bags, and started to demolish the camp not leaving a trace of our presence except for some 'golden snow'. (If you have not guessed, golden snow is produced when you have a piddle.) This exercise was organised with military precision. Every piece of equipment had its place on one of the three sledges.

When everything was aboard, we hit the trail and continued through the mountains in search for the hunting grounds. The white frozen scenery was spectacular as it glistened in the sun, but within an hour, everything changed as we could see a storm brewing in the distance. Andrew was not happy at all, and after a further ten minutes, he decided to return to our first camp as the storm was moving very fast towards us and even with his expert knowledge, he would not be able to guide us through the eye of the storm. It was too thick a storm as any landmarks were as any landmarks to speak of, which were scarce at the best of times were no longer visible.

This time it was our first priority to erect the tents even before he laid out his dogs. He told me that his dogs would endure the blizzard but we wouldn't. Once we had the tents up, Andrew had latched the dog chain to the ice we set to tying down the dogs. It had to be done so quickly that he even allowed me to help. No sooner than they were attached to the chain they curled up tightly whilst sitting on their legs to reduce to their bodily contact with the snow.

I took one last look at them before entering the tent. I really felt sorry for the dogs, but Andrew assured me that the dogs were used to this inclement weather and would be able to endure it for several days. It was only ten-thirty, but we would be there until the storm abated and none of us knew how long this would be. Although none of us were tired, we decided to get into our sleeping bags as they were the warmest place to be, even if we didn't fall asleep. I used the time to learn more about the Inuit culture and history from Andrew with Roland helping with the translation.

The Inuit territory was exclusively north of the Arctic treeline. The most southerly Inuits were part of the Rigolet community which were the first Inuits to come in contact with the first Europeans who were the first Vikings, who had also settled in Greenland. They were the first people to bring foreign disease which wiped out several distinct groups of Inuits. After about 1350, during what is known as the 'little ice age', the climate grew steadily colder and the Inuits in the high Arctic had to abandon hunting for Bowhead whales and move further south and lost a very important part of their diet.

The Inuits still speak one traditional language called 'Inuktitut' and is mainly spoken in Nunavut, English is the popular language, although their native tongue is still taught in schools and used around the home.

Andrew told me how they used to catch whales at sea as a group of different tribes armed only with harpoons which were made out of the ivory narwhale tusks which had been carved to a point with a sharp barb. These were attached to a float made out of a full seal pelt by a rope made from sinew and dried intestines. When several harpoons were thrown deep into the whale, the floats prevented them from diving until they eventually died from exhaustion. They made single passenger boats called qajaqs made from whale bones and covered in seal skins. These were extremely buoyant and could be easily righted by a single person, even if they were completely overturned, but how they did not immediately die from freezing to death in the ice-cold water is difficult to understand. The design of these boats has been coppied by the Europeans and are now called kayaks.

In those days as much as possible was harvested from the sea, and in summer, they killed caribou, musk ox, and birds. Their diet was rich in protein and very high in fat from seals, walrus, and whale blubber. Unlike us, they ate a very low carbohydrate diet, but vitamin 'c' was obtained from the raw meat such as the ringed seal and 'muktuk', whale skin, but how they chewed it is anybody's guess. We talked for hours. I was never tired of listening. Andrew was so pleased that I wanted to learn how the Inuits live now and have lived in the past...Andrew never got tired of telling me but even with Rolands help at times it was difficult.

Andrew like the rest of the Inuits were a very proud race but did not like all the changes caused by the influence of the "white man " and the new rules that they have imposed on them.

I like to listen to a storm at home when you lie there in bed all snug and warm and it was even nicer here as it blew across the tent, so long as the tent stood its ground I was quite happy. It was a thrilling experience, and added to the excitement, we all wished that we could have continued with journey and so long as the blizzard blew over fairly quickly, we would not have lost too much time. It was inevitable that we all fell asleep, and we did to the last man. I was the first to wake up. It was three o'clock, so I decided to put some ice in the pan to make a pot of coffee, but in the process, I woke Roland, who was sleeping next to me. Once it was brewed, I woke Andrew who was at the time snoring lightly but was pleased that I had decided to wake him.

He put on his boots which were the ones his wife had made him out of seal and caribou skins, using the seal skin as the inner lining with the hair inwards making them a very warm pair of boots, far warmer than mine and a fraction of the cost. He then unzipped the tent to look outside. He said that the weather had improved, but he would still prefer to leave it for a few hours before making a decision whether we should move or stay put. Andrew went for a chinwag with Qamayuq, probably to see what he would do in these circumstances, and when he returned after an hour or so, he said that we would stay there at least until we had eaten dinner and would probably stay the night. It was still very peculiar to me to say night when it wasn't and would not be dark which we call 'night'. I think it would be easier if I described the time on a twenty-four-hour clock and not refer to day or night. This is really difficult to get your head around. You really need a different mindset because when he says, stay the 'night', there isn't a night and a day as it is twenty-four hours daylight. Time is dictated by when and what you eat. It's bacon for breakfast, a cold snack for lunch, and a hot-cooked meal in the evening, so what he was saying was that he would decide what to do after our hot meal.

As we were now settling down for a good few hours, I suddenly thought of asking Andrew if he would teach me how to build an iglu. This would be a fantastic and constructive way of filling in the time while we were waiting for the weather to improve. I got a brilliant and positive response and saw his face light up with a smile. He was very pleased that I had asked him and said that it was his pleasure to teach me. It was now very firmly decided that we weren't moving today, so it is time for me to go to school.

'Come on, Dave, get your boots on, let's get started.' He unzipped the tent and walked across to his sleigh and lifted the tarpaulin to look for his knife. It was very similar to a machete and was protected by a scabbard made from caribou leather. I quickly put my boots on and joined him outside.

He had already started to look for suitable snow by thrusting his knife into the snow to find the best compacted snow to use to make an iglu. He could gauge the depth and density of the snow by how the knife felt in his hand and soon found the kind of snow he was looking for. The most difficult part was to remove the first two or three blocks to to form a rectangular hole, to enable him to "bottom out ". It was easy to cut the blocks of firm snow and back of the blocks, but you had to have space to cut the bottom of the blocks. Once this was made, you could fairly rattle them out, and he could lay them as fast as I could cut them, in fact even faster.

Compacted snow is a fantastic medium to work with. Just think about it, with a swathe of your knife, you can trim it down if it is too long, you can cut whatever angles you require, and you don't need any cement to join the blocks together either. My brickies at home would think they were in heaven if blockwork was as easy as it is here.

Andrew first marked out a circle to the size of igloo he wanted to build and laid his first row of blocks by cutting them with a slight angle leaning them inwards. Once the first ring was completed, he started the second row with an angle on the bottom to continue the inward line, but he also made them wedge-shaped which turned the overall construction into an upward spiral as it snaked around the circle. All the time Andrew was working from the inside of the igloo and had locked himself in, so after five courses high, he need to come outside to show me how to cut the snow blocks for the next stage. He decided where to make the door which was on the opposite side of the prevailing wind, and with a quick flash of his knife, he had made the door and crawled outside.

He showed me how to make the next blocks and then returned to the inside of the iglu to complete it. He needed an experienced hand for the final two rounds, so he shouted for Roland to come and help. They quickly capped off the iglu; all that was left to do now was to make a tunnel for entrance and to fill in the cracks to make it wind proof.

It had taken us less than an hour from start to finish, and we had made an iglu which would last until the summer when it would melt away. It was a great accomplishment for me, and I felt really coughed about it. This had been a totally unexpected event, and there was even more to come as we continued our, conversation, where we left off, in the igloo. (English spelling)

Before we crawled inside the iglu for our chat, Andrew wanted to explain how he would make a quick iglu, if you were caught up with a storm which was advancing quickly towards you and you needed to make an iglu in a hurry for protection. The quickest way was to build your iglu around your snow block quarry. Instead of building the iglu away from where you were cutting the blocks of snow, you use your quarry as part of the construction and once you have cut out one course of bricks and laid them, you were already two blocks high. This speeds up the construction of your iglu. You are building it both up and down at the same time, and therefore, when it is finished, you crawl down into it as though it is an underground cave with only half of it being exposed to the storm. Saving time on building it, this could be the difference between life and death because unlike the dogs, man would struggle to survive in the open in one of those blizzards.

It really was a cosy atmosphere inside the iglu, and even though we did not have anything on the floor, we all felt comfortable and quite warm. I could picture a family of Inuits living in there, sitting around a fire and eating, while dad was explaining how he killed the big white bear. Andrew told me that his father was a renowned hunter and was the only Inuit that had killed three polar bears with three different weapons. One with a harpoon, another with a knife, and the last one with a rope made from sinews. He must have been a very brave man. I for one would not like to be that close to a polar bear when I attempted to kill one.

White man has intruded on the Inuit society and brought in his rules, changing the Inuits' lifestyle forever. Instead of being totally self-sufficient, the Inuit people are now dependant on imported goods for all parts of their lives. Andrew explained that in his life, the basic pillars of Inuit culture and their heritage had been eroded away and were now gone forever. Their children now learn about what life used to be like, which is far away from how life is now. This is why Peter is teaching today's children about how their grandparents lived and survived, how they made their tools, iglu, and tents and their crafts like carving and sewing clothing.

The biggest single change which has had a knock-on effect to many others is that until the very recent past, the Inuit people were semi-nomadic following the foods supply with the seasons. In summer, they lived in tents and followed the caribou or musk ox, with the women gathering berries, tubers, leaves, and herbs. When they had exhausted the food supply around them and started to travel further afield, they shut up shop and moved camp. They also used to make another boat, an umiaq, or woman's boat. They were twenty to thirty-nine feet long and had flat bottom so they could sail close to the shore. They were made with wooden frames and covered in seal skins and were used to transport people, dogs, and the rest of their clutter, but unlike us, this was kept to a minimum. When you are nomadic, there is only room for the essentials. Some years they moved once or twice and occasionally they did not need to move at all. While the men fished and hunted, the women made clothes and boots using skins and a needle made from bone and using sinews or gut as cotton, all in preparation for the winter ahead.

In the winter months, they lived in an iglu built in exactly the same way that Andrew had just shown me. They kept themselves warm by wearing several layers of clothes made from leather and skins from the animals they killed and from a small fire which was more like a lamp, using oil squeezed and extracted from the fat and blubber of seals, whales, and walruses. The men hunted for seals and polar bears which were to be found on the frozen sea, just where we were going to hunt.

As semi-nomads, they sometimes travelled hundreds of miles, and there was another part of their life which is not commonly talked about. There were no doctors, hospitals, or care homes, and a tribe could only move as fast as the slowest member. It was the survival of the tribe that was imperative and not the individual. Elderly, permanently ill, and those with major accidental injuries were a liability to the clan, and death of these individuals by suicide was common place among the Iglulik Inuit. By ensuring that they died a violent death, Inuit elders purified their souls for the journey to the afterworld. People who needed assistance with their suicide made three requests to relatives for help. Family members would try to dissuade them, but with the third request by a person, assistance became obligatory. Andrew had given some brief and gruesome details about this part of nomadic life which was difficult enough for the fit and able, and without their support, these ones would never survive. I did some research on this when I got home, and there were various reports about it, but from what I learnt, senicide did go on.

On occasions, they would meet other tribes who lived outside the Arctic circle and in mainland Canada, who had themselves come into contact with white settlers who in turn had changed their lives. They exchanged information and stories about themselves, and these intermediaries gave them the introduction to the new white settlers at the Hudson Bay Company who would exchange skins, furs, and ivory from the walrus and narwhale for knives, axes, nails, and timber. You have got to remember that there are no trees within the Arctic Circle, and it's a resource and commodity that we take for granted but has never been a part of their life.

Once they learnt about it, they could see some of the benefits and started to exchange some of their excess skins and furs for Western goods. Slowly but surely, the influence of white society started to affect their lives in a real way because with access to timber and other building materials, they could make permanent homes and put roots into the ground. This together with transportation other than by dog and sleigh, firstly by vehicles and later also by snowmobiles made distances appear shorter and enabled them to go back and forwards to the hunting grounds on a daily or weekly basis.

However, the adoption of these new goodies has a cost; they were previously totally self-sufficient. They either didn't know about or need snowmobiles, housing materials, fuel for houses, clothes, or mobile telephones, but now, somehow they had to earn money to pay for these luxury items and do not have many resources at hand to do so.

We really had an in-depth conversation about the past, present, and the future, and I was inspired and even more excited about the rest of the trip. With ears alert, I could have listened for hours, but then Roland said that it was time for him to start making dinner and left the iglu.

Andrew and I were alone once more. He said that the changes to their society were inevitable, but he was not happy and felt that he was no longer in control of his life any more and at times it is very stressful. The Canadian government had imposed so many rules on them which by law they had to follow even if they went against their own practices and culture which had seen them right for generation upon generation.

The smell of the dinner drifted into the iglu, and as we were about to leave, I asked Andrew one more favour, which was whether I could sleep in the iglu. His first reaction was to say that it would be far too cold, but when Roland told him that this was an opportunity for me to have another Inuit experience and one not to be missed and that moreover if I was cold, I could come back into the tent, he gave his approval.

Dinner that night was a caribou steak with wild mushrooms which had been picked and dried in the summer, along with seaweed Inuit bread and wild berry sauce made by Andrew's wife.

Now that Andrew had wet my appetite and stimulated my interest in Intuit history, folklore, and culture, there was never a moment of silence again. At times, it was difficult to understand what Andrew was saying, but when Roland was there, it became a very interesting history lesson full of happy moments in all three of their lives. We had talked so long that none of us had even looked at the time or showed any signs of tiredness, but it was well past bed time and I still had to get my bed ready in the iglu.

Andrew tried one last time to put me off 'sleeping outside', or that was how he put it, as he now views sleeping in the iglu as outside and presumably sleeping in the ultra-modern tent as inside. However, he knew that I was not going to be persuaded to stay in the tent and came to ensure that I had prepared the floor correctly, which incidentally I had not, as I'd put one layer of skin's hair down instead of hair up which would have made all the difference to the insulation value and let the cold floor chill me. Once he was satisfied that everything was shipshape, he said sleep tight and closed the door with a big slab of a snow block. This was another bonus for the hunt, just fancy that I was going to sleep in an iglu and most importantly, one that I helped to build.

It took absolutely ages for me to fall asleep as I was so excited and lapping up and enjoying myself as a kitten laps up and enjoys its bowl full of milk. I woke up in a hot sweat and straight out of a wet dream. I dreamt that I was lying there totally naked on the warm seal skins, with a beautiful Inuit girl with long black hair. She was also totally naked. She was kneeling on top of me riding me for all she was worth as an Apache rides bareback on his horse. She was fucking me as I had never been fucked before. As she looked down on me with a satisfying smile and I looked at her face and into her eyes, it was a giveaway. Those eyes were not the eyes of an Inuit girl; they were the eyes of Megan. No one in the whole of the world has eyes like hers; it was unmistakably Megan in the guise of an Inuit girl. Even though we were thousands of miles apart, Megan was close beside me. I thought about her everyday but had not been this close to her for well over a week, and now I was missing her like hell. As I lay there thinking about her, I started to make up a poem to tell her when I arrived home.

It's quarter past midnight,
The evening has gone,
So I've got 'till the morning,
To write a love song,
My eyes are wide open,
I can see you by my side,
But I've only been dreaming,
And my dreams,they have lied,
You lay there beside me,
Your legs crossing mine,
It just seems like yesterday,
Since we were entwined,
But now that I 've woken,
And you're not there to touch,
My mind it is broken,
And my heart bleeds too much.

The storm had blown over while we were sleeping, and after breakfast, we packed up the camp, loaded the dogs, and continued the journey towards the frozen sea. This last stretch through the mountains played havoc with my back as each vertebra seemed to grate against each other when we hit every bump or ridge of ice. Even though I was now kneeling down trying to reduce the shock waves, I could not stop the piercing pain which was like a red-hot needle penetrating my spine. I would have to find a solution as it would be a further seven hours with only one stop for coffee and to stretch the old legs before we descended from the pass and down to the frozen ocean. I decided to try a spell standing outside the cabin and to holding on to it. All I would have to worry about was the wind chill on my face, but most of it would be covered in any case.

I thought again about offending Andrew as he had spent a lot of time and trouble making the cabin for me but realised that I would be no good to him if I damaged my back and was unable to hunt. I was still using the cabin to protect me from the wind, so his efforts were not all in vain. It was a crisp, clear day and the views were magnificent. There was not a cloud to be seen in the blue sky, and I could not wait to get going. I had caught a big dose of Arctic fever, not literally, and I was enjoying every single moment.

When we eventually reached the highest point in the pass and looked down onto the frozen sea, the horizon was miles and miles away; truthfully, it was so far away that you could not see where the sky met the ocean. Apart from its vastness which itself was very awesome and impressive, your senses were alerted to the tranquillity. There was not a whisper of wind, and the sheer silence was stunning. The cold, fresh air was so pure, clean, and being so cold, it was a most peculiar feeling as it entered my lungs. As we stood there, it was as though life itself had stopped, which in its own way was quite an eerie feeling. We all took time out to absorb the atmosphere which was different to anything that I had ever seen before and made me wonder how Andrew was going to navigate us around this expanse and eventually guide us back to this mountain pass without either a compass or a GPS and no signposts or beacons in sight.

To my great delight, the first sign of life we saw was a mother polar bear with two cubs who had only recently emerged from their winter den. They were some distance away, but I was so excited about seeing my first wild polar bears that Andrew unhitched the dog sledge from the skidoo, told me to jump on with him, and we set off to have a closer look. The others did the same and soon followed us. The tranquillity which I had enjoyed so much was immediately broken by the noise from the skidoo, which was totally alien in this prestige environment, when we were at full throttle and going at full speed across the ice. The mother bear would never have seen anything like this in her life before and made a bolt for it, but when her cubs could not run at her pace, she stopped to wait for them to catch her up. Andrew drove to within 100 yard of her, and we also stopped and let her settle down with her cubs. Andrew later took me closer to her to take a few photographs, and now, she did not seem to mind, but as we did not want to cause her anymore stress, we left her in peace to enjoy the new daylight with her cubs.

We were now heading away from the mountains and looking towards the horizon which we could not see from the top of the mountains, but now we were on the same level we found it, but it was still a long ways off. I could see Andrew's head moving from side to side as though he was looking for a lost penny which he must have found as he suddenly stopped and walked off to the right. He signalled to me to follow and shouted to Roland and Qamayuq who went to Andrew's sledge and unpacked his rifle. That is actually an over-generous term to say the least, it is better described as some sort of weapon, a single rusty metal barrel strapped on to a piece of wood in the rough shape of a stock with electrical tape and the sinews of some type of animal and it goes without saying it had no sites; thankfully, he only used it at point-blank range. I guessed what he had found. It was the breath hole of a seal which he knew was still using because there was no ice. When the sea is frozen over, the seals have to keep several breath holes open by visiting them regularly and breaking the thin ice, so that they can come up for air, and on many occasions, they use it to escape from a predator either from above or below the ice. Andrew knew that he should not have to wait too long as they surface at each hole on a regular basis. Andrew sent Roland and Qamayuq to get their weapons and find some other holes which the seals were using in the same area.

It is not an easy job. You have to stand immediately above it without moving a single muscle as the slightest movement will be picked up by a seal and it will use another breathing hole and you would have missed your chance. Once I had seen the hole, Andrew asked me to go back to my castle on the sledge as I might scare it off. They all stood motionless for over half an hour and I really do mean totally still without moving a single hair. I don't to this day know how they did it. I certainly could not have done, but I swear to you I saw this repeated time after time during our hunt, they were the most patient of men.

Andrew said that he wanted to continue for about another hour and then we would make camp. I didn't mind as I had been resting my bad back and giving it some light exercise as I was moving around to keep warm. True to his word, we stopped on time and we started to make camp, this time I was part of the team and would be so from now on. As yet I was still not allowed to help Andrew with the dogs, but I was confident that would come in time.

Meanwhile, Roland and I had a good time erecting our tent and laying the floor, and this time I got everything the right way up. I then went to chop up some ice to make the brew and help Roland get started with the meal which was caribou, the same as last night. We had a cup of coffee after the meal and then retired to bed as it had been a tough old day and all of us were tired. Even though it was minus thirty or so outside, we all stripped off to our last layer when we got in our sleeping bags. I remembered to put the linings of my boots in bed with me, just as Joe had said, 'It really is very important that your feet are warm. If you have cold feet, then the rest of your body is cold. This is the single most important thing about keeping warm in Arctic conditions. Take care of your feet.'

I slept right through and was woken again by Andrew who passed me a hot cup of coffee as he woke me. It really was five star service. Breakfast this morning was pancakes and walrus sausages which had a rather fishy taste and were very greasy but with the help of more than one large mug of coffee, they went down the hatch without too much trouble.

The good news this morning was that we weren't moving camp today as Andrew wanted a rekey on the area to see what activity there was.

This was the beginning of the hunt, no more snowmobiles. This is for real, and we were going to use the dogs and they knew it too. Roland and Qamayuq brought around the dog sleigh. They immediately began jumping up and down barking and yelping so loud that it was difficult to hear ourselves speak. They went frantic running backwards and forwards with such force that two of them broke away from the chain which made the others bark for even louder. Andrew was preparing the leads and harnesses which attach the dogs to the sleigh. He caught the two dogs which had escaped from the chain and gave them the back of his hand before tying them up again.

As the dogs were tied to the chain in a special sequence, it was a similar procedure when he harnessed them to the dog sleigh. He firstly removed their collars and then fitted them into their individual harnesses which were designed in such a way that when they pulled, all the weight was transferred from the strength in their shoulders directly to their legs giving them the maximum power for the least effort.

The lead dog was the first to take up his position at the front of the pack. I watched as Andrew put him in his harness and then onto the sleigh. I was even allowed to help a little, Roland unleashed them from the chain and then I took them to Andrew who put their harness on so that he could attach them to the sledge. The rest of the dogs sat whimpering until it was their turn and they knew when it was coming as they stood up when Roland approached them. They just couldn't wait to go to work.

Once the last dog was in place, Andrew cracked his whip and we were off and away. This was going to be a most spectacular journey. It aroused every sense in my body. On the dog sledge, you were very close to the ground which made me feel that I was going faster than I really was, eleven dogpower was generating a speed of maybe twenty miles an hour which was pretty good going. The closest comparison to it was probably when I was driving a go-kart where your sitting position relative to the ground level is similar and increases your perception of driving at a high speed.

Andrew had tied a rope across the sleigh for me to hold onto and you needed this to keep your balance as the sleigh veered first to the left and then to the right. As the passenger, I was directly behind Andrew on my knees and holding onto the rope. In order to keep my balance, I just couldn't sit there as a lump of clay, I had to actively ride the sleigh as though we're skiing, transferring one's weight from side to side as the ground conditions changed. When we first viewed the frozen ocean from the mountains, it looked like a totally flat plain of snow without any character and featureless, but in reality at this level it was far from that. When the winds did blow, they whipped the snow up into small ridges which froze and then when it snowed again, it covered them over to make everything appear flat again, in much the same way that the sea changes the sand on the ebb of each tide except the frozen snow ridges are constantly growing and a permanent feature until the summer thaw came, when all the snow and ice returns to the sea. The topography was quite deceiving, and it was not until the sleigh hit the ridges and violently veered up at forty-five degrees that you were aware of them and realised that the top of the ocean was far from flat. This is when the rope really counted as you hung on for dear life and quickly shifted your specific gravity to keep your balance, by passing your weight through your arms and clenching onto the rope.

Andrew was well used to this and took his guidance from the lead dog who intuitively knew from its years of experience where to look out for the pitfalls and tried to avoid them as best as it could, but even the dog got it wrong at times. This was not just a hunting expedition. It felt like a sport in the winter Olympics; you had to work very hard to avoid falling off. It was very, very exciting and an invigorating rip-roaring ride, causing my adrenalin hit a high causing my blood to race around my body and making my hair stand on end and giving me the most exhilarating sensation. I fell in love with this mode of travelling and got excited as much as the dogs every time we harnessed them.

Andrew was always scanning the ice and could pick out a bear miles away with his naked eye. At every vantage point, he would stop and take out his telescope to have a more detailed look. Each time he found one, he would firstly assess whether it was a male or female. This was easy to do as the females more often than not would have cubs. He then nearly always passed me his scope for me to have a look which may sound a very simple task but trying to find a white polar bear against a white snowy background is not easy. If I was having difficulty finding it, he would find the bear in the scope, then keeping it very steady, he would move his head to the side and allow me to look. When I still was unable to spot the bear, he would realign the scope again and again. I hate to admit it but sometimes I said that I could see the bear, when I had not a clue where it was, just to save any embarrassment on my part.

As we were hunting towards the horizon, we were at the same time gradually moving closer towards the open sea. Even though it was still hundreds of miles away, it still had an impact on the structure of the ice. The frozen sea is not one solid piece of ice but is made up of massive plates of ice, some for hundreds of miles, each piece pushes against each other and they are constantly moving even though we may not be able to see them move.

As we progressed, the scenery began to change, and it was a dramatic change at that, the easiest way to describe it is for you to imagine tipping a large bucket of ice cubes onto a table and then tipping a second bucket of ice cubes on the top of that. In some places, you will have the ice three or four blocks high, some will be on there sides, some will be on there ends, some will be laid diagonally and some on there tips leaning against another ice cube. Looking at the whole picture from above, it will look like a maze with pathways where there are no ice cubes, which makes glassing these areas very difficult indeed, first you see it, now you don't.

We all had our binoculars, and if we found a good vantage point, we could spend anything up to an hour just glassing before moving on to a new observation site where we would again start looking for that illustrious bear. This was repeated hour after hour and day after day. Andrew had the patience of Jobe and would constantly look through either his binoculars or telescope all the time, whereas the rest of us would take time off for a chat.

After two nights at this camp, Andrew decided that we should move on again to a new area, all that we were finding here was females with their cubs. He said that the males must be closer to the open water and that is where we would have to go if we wanted to find a good male.

Everything was loaded back onto the main sledges. Roland, Qamayuq, and I lifted the dog sleigh onto his sledge, while Andrew started to move the dogs from their chain and into their private travelling compartment; as usual we had their synchronised chorus to accompany us which was a nice change from the total silence as we did not have any form of music out on the sea ice.

I had adapted my new way of travelling by tying a rope over the cabin to use as a hand grip. This was a further improvement which made it very easy to keep my balance and totally removed the back strain which I sustained whichever way I sat in the cabin; this was to become my sole way of travelling. With the wind chill factor taken into account, it must have been well below minus forty degrees centigrade, but the penalty of being exposed to the elements was far outweighed by the benefit of avoiding any damage or pain to my back. I felt so inspired by the scenery and now I had 360-degree vision. It was a challenge to spot a bear before Andrew had seen it, although it was totally unrealistic to think that I had any chance of finding a bear before he did even though he had to look and drive the snowmobile at the same time.

There was not much of my face exposed if I wore my balaclava and also covered it with my gloves and the rest of my body was shielded by the cabin. The skidoo was probably eight or nine times as fast as the dogs and to avoid falling out I still had to ride it as though I was skiing, the rope that I tied to the sledge and over the roof of my cabin to hold onto was working well. This was by far the most comfortable way of travelling, and although you were standing all the time, it was sure better than crouching down inside the cabin and what's more you had a better view into the bargain. I would stand there as happy as a cock on a midding, chewing away at my almonds and kumquats.

The time passed fairly quickly, and after a couple of hours, Andrew stopped for what I thought was going to be a coffee break, but it wasn't. He had spotted some more breather holes and we really needed to kill a seal as the dogs had not eaten since we left Arctic Bay, which was five days ago. They all started to look for breather holes while I sat on the snowmobile sipping a mug of coffee, for all I could tell they could have been three statues, silent and totally motionless. Time just does not matter in this situation, and it has less meaning here than at home because there are no breaks in the day with dawn and dusk and without your watch each minute would be followed by another minute which would be followed by another hour which would be followed by yet another day. Living with constant daylight not only takes some getting your head around but totally disrupts your normal daily routine as you don't have a regular sleeping or eating times and sleeping in particular becomes even more difficult. I have nothing but praise for the guys. They stood waiting for a seal to return to clear its blowhole, but their dedication was to no avail and after half an hour, Andrew decided to move on.

When we are travelling for a long time, I never get board as such but my mind drifts away at its own leisure, dreaming and writing poetry or songs. I had just started writing a song when Andrew stopped again. He had seen another blowhole or an 'aglu' as it is called in their language. I could see that he was getting frustrated as we were not having any luck in shooting a seal to feed the dogs and if we were not successful soon, we would have to give them some of our food. They all were quick to find a hole that was in use and the waiting game started all over again. I was sitting, relaxing, and waiting when Roland called me over to his blowhole and asked me to watch and wait motionless. Then he passed me his rifle and said he was going for a dump. I'm a little deaf and with my hood up was not too sure if I heard him correctly, so I asked him to repeat it. 'Going for a dump.' I am probably stupid, but I really didn't know what the hell he meant. It didn't click at all, and I asked him if I could come too. I looked vacantly at him while he explained that he wanted to go for a shit. Now I understood why he wanted to go alone.

It was now my turn on watch. Me waiting over an aglu for a seal to appear 18.) I hoped that I could stand motionless and with beginner's luck, it might be me, who shoots the seal. Roland did not return to take over the sentry post, but after his 'dump' went back to the snowmobile to have a drink leaving me to continue until Andrew decided that it was time to pack in and move on to where he wanted to make camp. While I stood on guard frigid and frozen and not being allowed to move a muscle, I finished my song.

For Everyone

From ashes to ashes,
And dust to dust,
Now that I'm dead,
I can't earn a crust,
There's no need to worry,
I'll be just fine,
In the land of milk and honey,
You don't need a dime,
It does not matter whether,
You're yellow, black or white,
God, says it doesn't,
And he's always right.
It does not even matter,
Whether you're Hindu, Muslem or Jew,
When you go to heaven,
He will welcome you too,
The rules, they are simple,
The rules they are few,
There is no more stealing,
No killing or rape,
So if you can't take the changes,
Then don't join the queue,
When Jesus asks you to heaven,
And you pass through the gate,
All your sins are forgiven,
And a new life you will make,
Negro, Natzi or Christian,
You'll all be best friends,
You are working for God now,
And his peace never ends,
So stretch out your arms,
He will welcome everyone in,
Now you've got life eternal,
And everyone wins.

As we set off towards our next camp, the cupboard was still bare and the dogs would remain hungry for at least another day. Andrew chose a very interesting site to make camp, beneath the shadow of a very big iceberg. This one had broken away from the glacier but hadn't made it to the open ocean before the winter freeze began and was land locked or I should say sea locked, until the thaw in the spring, when it would once again be free to roam until it eventually thawed out and melted away.

As a four-man team, making up camp was now a doodle. We all knew the routine like the back of our hands. Once Roland and I had erected our tent, Andrew let me help him with the dogs, which was a great privilege as his dogs are very special to him.

That night's meal was Arctic charr accompanied by more Arctic charr and bread. I'm not complaining. I wanted to live like an Inuit, eat like an Inuit, and hunt like an Inuit and was thoroughly enjoying every minute of every day. After our meal, Andrew set off on his snowmobile to check out the ice and decide which direction we would go with the dogs later on. He said that he could hear and smell some open water. His senses were truly remarkable and gave me total confidence in his ability to find our way without a map in this ever-changing wilderness. Andrew was only away for around an hour, and when he returned, we immediately started to harness the dogs to their sledge.

I would love to say that we set out on a lovely evening and had a fantastic sunset while we were hunting, but we didn't; it was a great hunt, but we had to skip the sunsets.

With the dogs ready and waiting, Andrew cracked his whip yet again and we were away towards a high spot he had found. This was where he had been and he had seen two females with cubs. They were strolling there and another female had joined them, as we stood there. The bears were close enough to see without any help, but when I looked through my Leica binoculars, it was a pleasure to the eye, I could see every hair on their bodies, every action the cubs made, and I could not take my eyes off them while they were playing together. Eventually we had to move on. The dogs pulled us along until we arrived at the best viewpoint of all. I called it ice cube mountain because that was exactly what it was. The movement of these massive plates of ice towards each other had forced the ice cubes up vertically and broken off even more making the mountain even higher. This is a force that you cannot see as it is so gradual, but you know that it is there, just as you cannot see hydraulic power in a machine and I know all about that. When I was in my young twenties, I was building our own house and was using an old model JCB which has a slew bar. I had got the bloody thin stuck and took a short cut. Instead of going back inside the cab to operate the controls, I stood with one foot on the slew bar and left the other dangling. When I was using the controls from outside, I pulled the wrong leaver; it brought a spike on the arm right into my leg, below the knee. The pain was instant and deadly. I reversed the lever to take the spike out of my leg. The doctor said that I was lucky, some fucking luck. If it had been two inches higher, we would have had no choice but to amputate my leg. I know at first hand what silent hydraulic power can do. It is not always wise to take the low road. It has the same result as it did in the race between the hair and the tortoise.

Some of these blocks of ice are at least twenty-foot long and the mountain itself would be over 150 feet high. Andrew was first to the top and had already started glassing before we reached him. It was not a difficult climb, but as you would expect, it was very slippery and in some cases it was two steps up and three steps down, like snakes and ladders. When we eventually got there, the view was tremendous and we could see for miles. Just beneath us there were another two females with their cubs. Andrew wasn't interested in females. He had one and only one objective and that was to find me a male polar bear in good condition that I could shoot. Wasn't interested is probably not the right word, he has a tremendous interest in all the wildlife around him, but at this moment, he was focused on finding me a male. As for me, I was more than happy to sit and watch the cubs playing together and to leave Andrew to his job. Inch by inch he covered the ground, and when he had checked out one area, he would cover it again to see if he had missed anything or anything that was hidden had now come into view.

Landscape that he was watching is what I described as though thousands of ice cubes had been thrown onto a table. A bear could be out of site and hidden behind a block of ice one minute and when you had passed that area, it would appear in a gap, so he had to check it again and again. He knew that there were bears around here and it was only a matter of time finding them. Meanwhile Roland and I were both content watching the mothers and cubs playing below us. Every second was a precious moment and I felt honoured to be able to watch them lying like any other baby in their natural environment.

Anyone reading this book who is not a hunter is bound to be at a loss to understand how I can get so much pleasure sitting for literally hours fully engrossed in the activities of the young bears playing together and yet when the opportunity arises, I will take my rifle and shoot one of these beautiful creatures. I must admit that at times I can't give an honest explanation to myself either, other than to say that hunting is a primeval instinct in mankind which in the past stems from the necessity to find food. This instinct is a very prominent part of my make-up and is still much the same in some other parts of the world where hunting and gathering is still an important part of their lifestyle and essential to their survival. However, in the majority of Westernised people, the desire to hunt is suppressed or of little or no importance. Although they are carnivores, there is no mental connection between the meat they eat and the animal it comes from.

It may also sound very silly, but I do get a lot of pleasure looking at my trophies and appreciating just how beautiful they are and how clever God and nature is to produce for example so many different sizes and shapes of antlers in different animals. To me it is an unbelievable feat of nature that a moose sheds its antlers every year, which can be up to five feet wide and weigh anything up to twenty pounds. Each year, its antlers get bigger and bigger until they reach a peak and then start to decline and regress as it is now out of the running as the dominant male and no longer needs them.

While we were relaxing and watching the polar bear show, Andrew had sent Qamayuq and Roland to go and hunt for a seal as it was becoming very critical. They came back with an empty bag yet again. Andrew and I were still glassing from the top of the ice-cube pyramid. I was totally enthralled watching the young polar bears playing; like all young offspring, they did not have a care in the world. I would never get tired of this and absorbed every drop of the atmosphere as it was so surreal. On the other hand, Andrew was endlessly searching for my bear, but all he saw was females, females and more bloody females. That's all that Andrew could find. He was now getting tired and his head must have been spinning with shear concentration, so he decided that Roland should have a turn with the telescope, while he took a break and went to try to get a seal. I asked if I could go with him, but he said in a nice way that it was very important and he would be better on his own. He went off on Roland's snowmobile which upset the dogs who had been lying sleeping peacefully awaiting for him to come down from ice cube mountain. Then when he did, they all stood up and started barking with excitement as they thought that they were going to work, but when he set off on the snowmobile, you could literally see the disappointment in their faces watching him disappear. When they realised that he was not returning, they eventually lay down or groomed themselves.

Like me Roland does not like scanning with the telescope. It's really hard work. I suppose I should have offered to help, but I preferred sitting and watching my bears and chomping on my almonds and kumquats. Andrew was away for a good hour and came back totally fruitless, seemingly the seals were playing by a different set of rules, as normally, he should have harvested one by now. We had not had any luck either, the males were being very elusive and obviously were going to make us work hard to find them.

Andrew decided that we were going to go a different way back to camp and took a detour which extended our journey by at least two hours, but what does this matter when you have all day and no one is checking the time. This was not a complete waste of time; much to the contrary, he could smell some open water and we soon had it within our view. It is strange and quite amazing. Suddenly you find open water amongst miles and miles of frozen sea, and it immediately makes you appreciate the dangers and understand how the underlying currents which you are not aware of influence what happens under the ice and the movement of the ice plates.

As we approached, Andrew lost his calm-collected spirit. As he turned around, his face was beaming with excitement and I knew why he was so pleased, we both had spotted five seals basking on some islands of ice floating close to the edge of the water. As we were travelling on the dog sledge, we were able to approach close to them without alarming them. They much prefer to lie on the floating islands rather than the sea ice as they cannot be reached very easily by the polar bears. The islands were anything up to fifty feet long, and they were all slowly moving towards a bigger stretch of open water, it was as though they were in a river. Andrew watched and picked out an island that appeared to be moving towards us. Qamayuq and Roland had arrived to help. Roland shot the seal in the head. It did not move an inch and surprisingly neither did any of the other seals. We knew it was dead as the blood ousted out of the wound staining the white ice. The island continued to move towards us but became blocked by several small ones which were in its path and prevented it moving any further. A second seal was shot which was slightly closer, but we were not able to land that one either, for some unknown reason, the current had changed. Luck was definitely not on our side, and it was not a very good omen for the dogs. They really can exist on fresh air, but the question that I wanted to ask was for how long. Andrew was getting very frustrated, nothing was working out for him, we couldn't find the male polar bears and couldn't get food for the dogs either. He decided very foolishly in my view to try to jump from one small island to another to reach the dead seal, which indicated to me just how serious the situation was. On the second jump, he slipped and slid across the ice. We knew how dangerous it was and persuaded him to abandon the idea and think of a different strategy. We decided to return to camp, and Qamayuq was going to make a grappling iron which we could use to try and hook the seal and pull it to the shore. Qamayuq knew exactly how he was going to make it and started immediately when we reached the camp. He started by removing three steel bars from a pan stand. These were about ten inches long and a quarter of an inch in diameter. He then set to filing a sharp point on each of them. Once they all were pointed, he knocked each of them into the wooden sleigh about three inches deep. This was the only way that he could hold them in order to bend them into a hook. These guys are really ingenious. They never give in until they have solved a problem. I suppose this is because all their lives and the lives of their forbears have always lived in very adverse conditions, and they have had to adapt their lives to fit, otherwise they would not have survived. This mentality stands them in good stead when problems do knock on their doorstep, and this situation we were in now is a prime example of what I mean.

Once Qamayuq had bent the hooks, he asked me to hold them in position while he bound them with sinew. He was making a treble hook similar to the ones I use when I'm fishing except thirty times larger. He used sinew because it tightens when it gets wet and would give a better grip on the steel, preventing it falling apart. As he was lashing it together, he built in a loop so that he was able to attach it to the rope. As soon as it was finished, we headed back to the dead seals to bring home the bounty.

Andrew followed by Roland and Qamayuq descended to the waters' edge only to find that the seals had moved further out and they had to cross several blocks of ice to get within range to be able to swing the treble around his head in circles, with an action similar to a Scotsman throwing a hammer, gathering up enough speed to be able to launch it towards the dead seal. The first throw landed over twenty feet away and bounced into the air when it hit the ice. He pulled the rope back in and repeated the action again and again, each time getting closer to the seal. Roland asked him if he could have a throw, and he seemed to have a better idea but still could not hit the target and neither could Qamayuq when it was his turn. I was sitting on a block of ice and shouted down to Andrew to ask him if I could have a throw as I was good at throwing the hammer, but he told me it was too dangerous and to stay where I was. I honestly don't know whether it was for my safety or he did not want me, the Scotsman to succeed where the three Inuits hunters had all failed.

I did however suggest that they change their technique which I thought would help; instead of rotating it around their head, they should swing parallel to their body and release it at the bottom of the circle. This immediately improved their action and brought the treble closer to the seal and it looked as though we were in with a real chance of harvesting the seal. As Andrew was pulling back the treble which had landed very close to the seal, one of the barbs lodged in the ice and the harder they pulled, the deeper the hook buried itself in the ice, at one time all three of them were trying to pull it out, but it had too good a hold and the island was too big to pull it closer. The Gods were really working against us and the more it did the more determined Andrew was to succeed. To my amazement, he picked up Roland's rifle and started to shoot at the sunken treble hook which was lodged into the ice. After the third shot, it was set free. They tried and tried to hook the seal, but in the end gave it up as a bad job and decided to return to camp to eat. At this point in time, eating was not Andrew's priority. He sent Roland and Qamayuq to go and fetch his snowmobile and sledge which carried the dog's mobile kennel, which we had left it behind when we changed to using the dog's sledge. They set off together on Roland's snowmobile so they could bring back Andrew's kit. I was curious why he wanted his sleigh back at camp as this was not in his original plan and I was totally gobsmacked when he told me what he wanted to do. I could hardly believe my ears and I don't think anyone else would either. He said that he was going to build a boat out of the dog's travelling compartment. I already knew that the Inuits were a determined, resourceful, and ingenious race, but this takes the biscuit, for one to attempt to build a boat in the middle of the frozen sea without hardly any hand tools. It had to be seen to be believed and I have the highest respect for Andrew's resourcefulness, but I was beat as to know how he was going to do it.

I was feeling a little tired. It had been a very hard day, and we had already missed our lunch and it looked like that we were going to have a long day ahead as Andrew was not about to give up before we had fed his dogs. I took Rolands rifle and went back to the open water to see what was happening. I could not believe my luck, there was a bearded seal on a small ice island onle twenty feet from the ice cap. I shot it in the head then went to tell Andrew. I was so tired that I went for a quick catnap while we waited for the guys to return with Andrew's sledge. Roland had already started to prepare the meal while I was asleep, and Andrew started to dismantle the dog sleigh and build his boat with the help of Qamayuq.

I was awoken by the smell of onions that Roland was cooking on the stove with some meat which I did not recognise, but Roland told me that it was whale meat and it would be another first for me. He told me to look outside and see how his dad was getting on with the boat. He had nearly had it finished and was putting the finishing touches to it. I was very surprised how quickly he had completed the boat and how strong it looked. It should be able to hold his weight before it sunk into the cold ocean taking Andrew with it. The problem that I could see is that it was not watertight and water would rush in through the joints.

Roland called us to come for our meal. I went in, but Andrew and Qamayuq said that they wanted to finish the boat first and resumed their work. The whale steak was excellent, this adventure was full of surprises. I really was enjoying being part of an Inuit family, we polished the diner off in minutes. I was waiting for the second helping of my favourite pudding of pancakes filled with berries when Andrew poked his head into the tent and said that 'the boat was hungry and wanted some pancakes for its dinner'. This was a very strange request, but Roland obliged and passed him the pan of batter as we followed him out of the tent to see what he was doing. The ingenuity of the man was astonishing and endless. I take my hat off to him yet again. He started to fill the joints on the boat with pancake batter to seal them. The batter was freezing insitu and closing the joints. He meticulously filled every joint and nail hole both internally and externally and then gave them a second coat for good measure. I thought that when the boat was in the water, the batter would dissolve opening up the joints, but I was wrong, it held tight and Andrew's boat proved that it was seaworthy.

We tied the boat onto the sledge and took it as close as possible to the open water where we hoped that the dead seals were still lying on the ice islands. We then had to manhandle the boat as best we could down to the open water. Andrew had made himself an oar and climbed into the boat but not before we tied a safety rope around his waist in case things went wrong and we had to pull him out of the sea.

It only took a few minutes to reach the seal that I shot and tie a rope around its flipper so that we could pull it back to the solid ice. At least now we had meat for the dogs, poor devils they had gone near to the limit of their endurance and were on their last legs at the brink of starvation. It did not take him very long to skin out the seal. This was a bearded seal and the only parts that the Inuit eat are the ribs, similar to eating ribs of pork, the blubber, and one parts of the intestine. The skin is kept for making shoes and harnesses for the dogs as it is extremely strong and durable.

Andrew chopped up the remainder of the seal and began to feed the dogs who knew that there was food on the table and were going frantic. It was a remarkable sight. They must have been in pain with hunger. There was an overpowering smell of blood and guts and they wanted part of it. Even feeding the dogs was not as straightforward as you would expect. Andrew had a special routine and distributed the quantity of the meat according to the dog's physical condition with some getting significantly more meat than others. It made me feel very happy seeing them eating at last. I still find it hard to believe that they can exist on such meagre rations and work so hard on an empty stomach, they are miraculous animals. These are Inuit dogs and worlds apart from the general public's conception of an Eskimo on a sledge being pulled by huskies which may be a romantic picture but nowhere near reality, and I can assure you that your typical everyday pet husky would not last a week or even a day in these freezing Arctic conditions with little food to eat. The modern Inuit dog they use comes from the Canadian Eskimo Dog. It is called a Quimmiq and has genes from the wolf, the Siberian Husky, and the Alaskan Malamute. The Inuit used to perform rituals to the newborn pups to give them favourable qualities, the legs were pulled to make them strong and the nose was poked with a pin to enhance their sense of smell.

We had left the boat tied to an ice rock on the water and Andrew wanted to go back and see if we could get the other seal as we did not want to run out of meat again, especially because this one was a grey seal and was good meat for us. When we got there, the islands had moved further away and the seal had gone with them drifting further away at a good rate of knots and did not look like stopping. It was too risky to go out in the boat to catch it. This again shows just how strong the currents are under the sea ice flow which you would never realise unless like us you saw the effects of the current first hand. You can see how quickly the ice plates can move together or apart. If Andrew had set off in his makeshift boat with only one oar, we might have never seen him again, and without him, I did not have a lot of confidence in the others to get me back to Arctic Bay. It took a lot more effort getting the boat out of the water up through the ice rocks and onto the sledge to take it back to camp, but with a lot of hot air and swearing which is the same in almost any language, we eventually succeeded in doing just that and then sat down to congratulate ourselves.

I could have easily downed a good pint of beer or even two or three, but we did not have any on board and had to settle for a mug of tea. The Inuits generally do not drink alcohol, although some of the younger ones are partial to an odd bottle of beer or even a wee dram. I had brought that special bottle of whisky which Pop had bought and had somehow remained intact and I was going to open it on my birthday or when I had shot the polar bear, whichever came first. With our luck so far, the latter seemed a long way off, and it wasn't for the want of trying as we were out glassing for over eighteen hours a day.

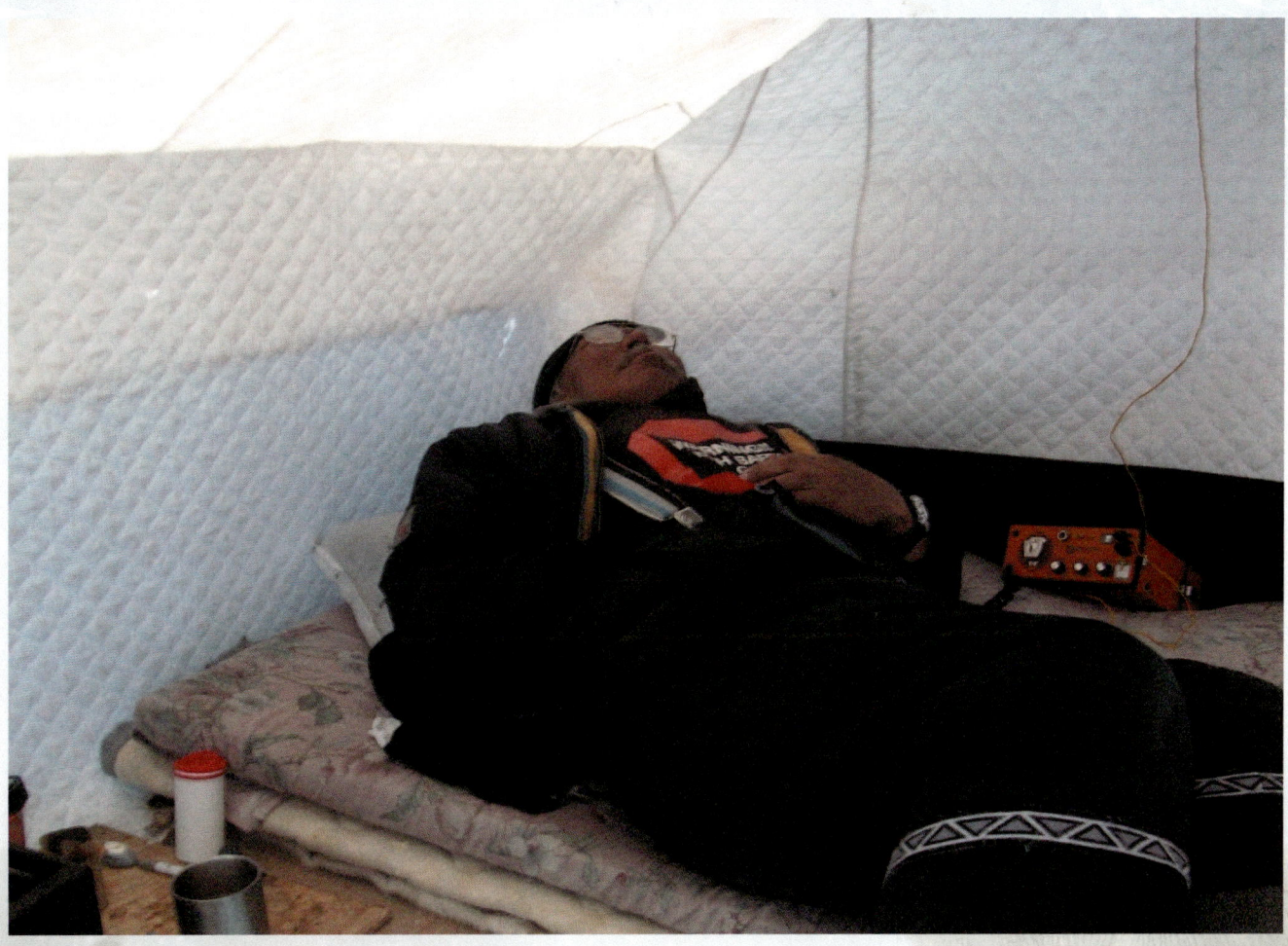

Andrew wanted to leave the dogs to digest their meal for another couple of hours before we left camp for another reckie, so he suggested that we went a walk and to look for tracks or maybe find an open breath hole and try to kill another seal which wouldn't go amiss. Even though we had a language problem, we managed to get by with sign language and his pigeon English, going a walk with Andrew was both interesting and enlightening. There was far more to be seen than I had expected, and as there had not been any newly fallen snow since we arrived, we were able to find a lot of polar bear tracks within quarter of a mile from our camp. These were focused in one particular area where the bears moved from the open ice into the area which had been covered in ice cubes and was like a maze. All had gone in at the same entrance to the ice cubes but gradually dispersed on different paths, making it easier for us to identify who was where. Andrew reckoned that there were three different females, two had two cubs and one had a single. When I asked him how he knew, he said that the one with a single cub

was easy as it only had the one cub, but if I looked carefully at the spoors of the cubs, then one pair of prints were significantly larger than that of the others. On the way back out, he spotted the spoors of an Arctic fox which often follow polar bears hoping to find some leftovers from a kill. I decided to cut out a footprint from the front paw and a hind foot to take back to show the lads. I was surprised because this was very easy to do and they'll looked pretty good. When the polar bear walks on a fresh fall of snow, he creates new footprints which because of his weight he exerts so

much pressure to consolidate the snow, and when it freezes, you can remove the footprint intact. I can remember making moulds of deer, fox, and many other animals using plaster of Paris when I was a young boy scout. It fascinated me then and these polar bear prints fascinate me now. The only difference is that because they are made of ice, I can't take them home with me, but it was still fun to do and I've got the photograph in any case.

Andrew decided to take a detour and check out the open water again, just in case the island with the dead seal had drifted into a better position for us to gather it before he dismantled the boat and rebuilt the dog kennel for the journey back to Arctic Bay, which was eventually inevitable as we were getting closer by the hour to the end of our hunt. I was enjoying myself so much, and with no distinction between night and day, it wasn't easy to keep track of each day and I wasn't counting them as they passed by. To my surprise, Andrew had been and he caught me by surprise the next day. I was relaxing in the tent when Roland unzipped the tent, popped his head in and said that his dad wanted to see me. I had been asleep and was still yawning as I left the tent, when to my surprise they all started clapping and singing happy birthday in Inuktitut. Then each of them came and gave me a big hug and wished me happy birthday. The last time that Andrew was in Ottawa visiting his wife who was seriously ill and in hospital, he had gone shopping and bought the letters to say 'happy birthday' which he now displayed before my very own eyes. That was just so thoughtful and kind of him, to think of my birthday at a time when he was worrying about his wife. That was not all either, he presented me with an arrow head which he had made as a gift that I will cherish and will keep forever.

It was a fair scramble through the ice blocks to get to where we expected to find the seal, and when we did eventually get there, the cupboard was bare. Andrew had to admit that we were not going to find it and that we have to make another kill. Our lost seal wouldn't be wasted as it would most likely be eaten by a hungry bear, they have exceptionally good noses and would be able to scent it from miles away and then swim out to the island to get it.

We had given ourselves a fair walk back to iceberg camp, but we weren't in a hurry and this was the first exercise that I had had since I arrived at Arctic Bay . The walk was certainly warming me up inside my Arctic clothing, but thankfully, I didn't break out into a sweat as it makes you very cold when you stop exercising. I was walking back five or six yards away from Andrew on a different track, and as I was looking down to avoid me tripping and falling on the ice, I noticed some more bear prints. They were from only one bear and were a lot bigger than the ones we were observing earlier. I called Andrew over to have a look. His face lit up when he saw them, and he gave me the thumbs up and a big cuddle. These were defiantly the spoors of a male bear. They confirmed that there was a male bear in the area. All we had to do was find it. Unfortunately, there was no high ground where we could get a good view of the area to see if we could see it. We would have to wait until we were back at the camp which was only five minutes away and climb to the top of the iceberg to scan the area. I threw away the footprints that I was carrying and cut out the tracks of the male bear to show the others when we arrived back at camp.

Roland and Qamayuq were there waiting for us to return. They had the stove on and quickly made us a nice mug of drinking chocolate, but Andrew wouldn't wait even a minute for his and set off with his telescope and tripod in his hands to climb to the top of the iceberg and look for the bear whose tracks we had found. Climbing the iceberg was in itself a skilled and difficult achievement, and I just can't overemphasise his dedication and determination. If there was a bear out there, he was going to find it come low or high water. As for me, there was no way that I was going to attempt to climb the iceberg, instead I drank my drinking chocolate, lay on my bed, and promptly fell asleep. I was out for the count and did not waken until Roland started to shake me. He had already tried shouting at me with no effect and had to resort to physical violence to get me to come around. Andrew was still on the top of the iceberg and wasn't intending to descend until he had found the bear. Roland shouted up to him that the dinner was ready and he would have to come down as he was not bringing it up to him. When he took the lid off the pan, the smell was truly awesome and it drifted up towards Andrew who had the nose of a bloodhound or I really say a polar bear as its nose is even more finely tuned. This immediately did the trick and he started to descend.

He could not resist fresh bearded seal for his dinner and came down in a jiffy.

Qamayuq had prepared the seal meat, and it smelled scrumptious. Roland asked me if I would prefer chicken instead and I had to reassure him that I much preferred to try the seal first. All three of them looked at me as though I'd gone out, as I dived into the pan with my fork, pulled out a large piece of breastbone, and started to eat it with my hands just like a true Inuit. When I returned to the pan for a piece of blubber, their faces were stunning, a cross between a violent shock and sheer amazement. They sat there staring straight at me with their bottom jaws dropped, as I opened my mouth and placed the blubber on my tongue. I like eating the fat from a lamb chop, beefsteak, or a piece of belly pork, as to me it has the more flavour than the meat, but eating this blubber was a totally different sensation and flavour. As I closed my mouth without either chewing or pressing it with my tongue, the oil started to ooze out of the blubber. It was a very thin oil and had a unique and distinctive flavour which I find very difficult to describe. It was neither fishy nor meaty. It wasn't bland and it wasn't overbearing, but it had a distinctive flavour that I really enjoyed and one that I will never forget. Once I did start to put some pressure on it between the roof of my mouth and my tongue, the oil continued to ooze out and be released until all you were left with was a light tissue which I can only describe felt as though you had a succulent ball of cotton wool in your mouth. The three Inuits sat there astound and had made no attempt to start their meal. They obviously preferred to watch me. Why, I don't know, it was not such a big deal to me, I think that they were waiting for me to try the intestine which I now was about to do.

This was really chewy with a strong fishy flavour which I did not immediately take to but wasn't so bad that it made me want to spit it out. The taste lingered in my mouth after I had swallowed it, so I quickly ate another piece of blubber which I had enjoyed. Roland asked me if I really had enjoyed it and I told him that if I hadn't, then I would not have gone back for more. I went back for the breast and the blubber and I don't think they noticed that I only had a second helping of the intestine.

I have eaten intestine before, in the UK sausage skins used to be made from pig's intestines, although most of them are now made from a synthetic material and the skin of a good haggis is from a sheep's stomach. The only true intestines that I have eaten previously werepigs intestines from a market stall in Venezuela where they barbecued it. The only difference is that they had not bothered to remove the contents beforehand, which you could probably pass as maize stuffing.

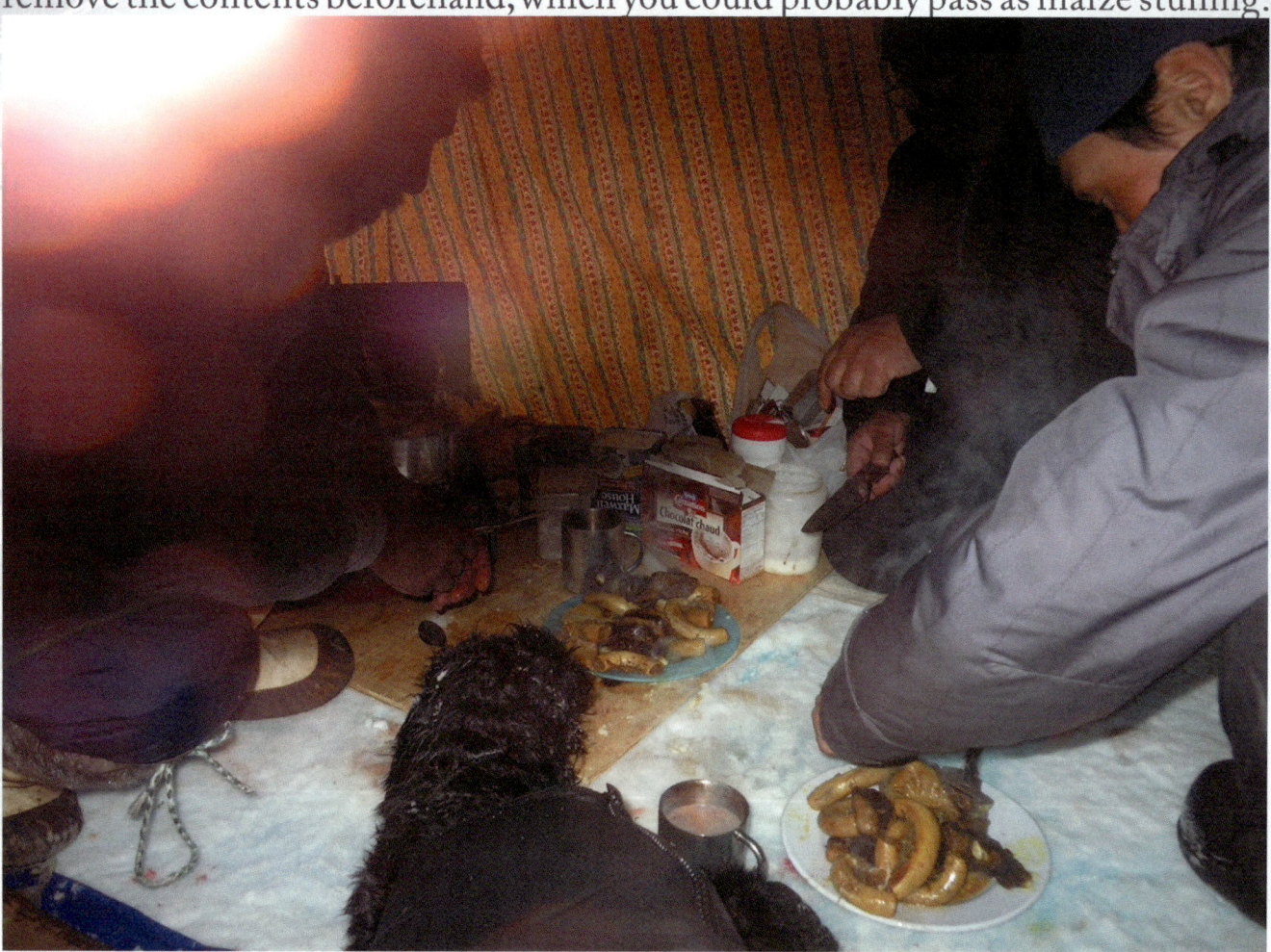

   With dinner eaten and over, it was now time to harness the dogs to the sledge and head off to ice cube mountain for the last time as we were going to go in a different direction the next day. I thought that I could start to see the strain in Andrew's face. This was one of the few occasions that he had not found a suitable trophy in the first ten days of a hunt and now time was passing fast, with only the spoors of one male which we had seen earlier today. He had sent the others out in different directions to scout, the polar bear numbers in this region were not suffering as we must have seen well over thirty different females with cubs at foot, in the small area where we had been hunting. However, the males were proving to be very elusive. Time was running out and I started to feel that the chips were down, the dice was not running in our favour. The dogs knew their way to ice cube mountain as they had been there several times before and we could see our previous tracks in the snow.

We stopped twice on the way at elevated positions to have a quick scan but neither was productive, so we continued to the base of iceberg mountain. As on previous occasions, Andrew gathered his telescope and tripod and climbed up to the summit continually hoping to spot a bear. I had caught sight of an Arctic fox and went off to stalk it and see if I could get close enough to be able to take a good photograph. I had followed it for more than a mile and was slowly catching up with it when the weather began to turn, storm clouds were gathering ahead of me, and the clear blue sky started to turn grey, so I decided to head back to Andrew. When I arrived, he was already waiting for me at the bottom.

He did not waste any time. I jumped on board. He cracked the whip and the dogs were on the move again.

We had got to head back fast or we could be caught in the middle of a snow storm without any shelter and that could give us some enormous problems and even prove fatal. If it did catch us, then Andrew might have to build one of his emergency iglus which although it may prove very exciting, it is not the scenario that either of us really wanted. I was in the

same position on the sledge as always, kneeling behind Andrew and holding on to the rope to keep my balance, but this time he was pushing the dogs as fast as they could run and they seemed to be just loving it. I wonder how fast they would have moved it they hadn't had that one meal but I don't suppose I'll ever know. We would be about a half hour from the camp and the iceberg had just come into sight when the storm caught us up. When I looked behind, the blue sky had totally vanished, replaced by grey clouds and falling snow with visibility down to less than a fifty yards. I had total confidence in Andrew's ability to get us back to camp, but I have to admit that I was getting a little scared. Dying is one thing, but if I had a choice, I would prefer not to die by being slowly frozen to death. All of a sudden we hit a frozen ridge and the sledge was thrown vertically four feet into the air. I accidentally let go of the rope and I landed with such force that I was thrown off the sledge into two feet of snow. It shuck me up, but I had a soft landing. It took Andrew a few minutes to slow the dogs down and turn them back around to come and pick me up. I was buried beneath the snow and he could not see me. As luck would have it, I wasn't injured in any way, and once back on board, it did not take very long to get the dogs back up to full speed. I had never expected any of this, when I first set out from home, racing on a dog sledge in an Arctic blizzard to beat a snow storm, just wasn't on the agenda.

As I arrived in Arctic Bay, a dog sledge race lasting for two full days was just departing and I'd lay a penny to a pound that had we entered it, we would have had a good chance of winning. We were still about ten minutes off camp and the visibility was getting worse as we could no longer see the iceberg. The dogs weren't relenting, powering away at full speed. Then one of the skis hit another ridge of frozen snow causing it to lean up at ninety degrees from the horizontal and looking as though it was going to overturn. This time I did not let go off the rope and we both leaned over against it to try to bring it back to the ground. It was then that I took a good look at the construction of the sledge which helped explain why it was so stable. If I had asked my joiner at home to make me a twelve-foot sledge, he would not know where to start but after a few hours, he would have the job done and would come for me to inspect it. Thinking that he had done a good job, he would tell me that it is as solid as a rock and would go anywhere, I've done a belt and braces job on this, it is bolted together as well as screwed and won't give an inch. Well, that was exactly what the problem would be, 'it would not give an inch'. On the other hand, Andrew's sledge was the exact opposite. There was not a nail, screw, or bolt in it. His sledge was lashed together with rope. He had drilled a series of holes at fixed intervals along the full length of each ski, the transoms were laid across the two skis and projected about two inches either side of the ski on its outer side at this point. The length of the transoms dictated the width of the sledge and you could have the two skis parallel or at a slight angle. He then had cut a notch on each side of the transoms which was used to lock in the rope as he tied them to the skis. This was repeated on both sides for the full length of the sledge which was the same principle they used when they made their sledges from whale bones and Arctic charr. Before the Inuits had access to timber, they used frozen Arctic charr and the baleen from the mouths of whales to construct their sledges. Instead of attaching some steel to the underside of each runner which is what we might have done, Andrew had used a length of three-inch alcathene water pipe which he had sliced open and forced over the wood to act as a runner and proved to be very good for the job. With this type of construction, his sledge was very flexible and so when one runner hit an obstacle, it was able to take the impact by bending while the other runner moved independently. If we were using our sledge, then the wood must most likely have cracked with the impact. The Inuits had certainly had developed the technique of lashing and binding of their sledges off to a fine art, and there had been no trouble with any of the sledges we were using for the whole of the hunt.

Bouncing up and down had given me a hell of a jaunt. My stomach felt like that it had been used as a boxer's punch bag and the rest of my body was just frozen with stress. Grasping hard on the rope and leaning over to change my balance was now instinctive, instant, and an automatic reaction which helped save the

day and fortunately this was the last incident before we arrived back at camp.

We were the first to return. I was quite worried about the others, but Andrew said that they have been in these kinds of situations before and not to worry. He had sent them the opposite direction and unlike us who had the storm catching us up from behind, they were heading towards the storm and would soon be back at camp.

Our first priority was to get the dogs off the sledge and back on the chain. This time he really appreciated my help and let me remove them from their harnesses while he tied them to the chain. I was untying the last dog when I heard the sound of the snowmobiles in the distance. They were approaching us fairly fast and would soon be back with us. I took the axe and went to fill the pan with ice so that I could have a hot drink ready for them when they arrived back at camp. This was a day to remember, it will forever be imprinted on my mind, and when I think of the Arctic, I will be able to relive the excitement of this day. I did, however, take the precaution of writing it up in my notes for good measure.

We did not have to ask them about their scouting as they were literally bubbling with excitement. They had found fresh tracks of not one but two male polar bears, and although they had not actually seen the bears themselves, this was a massive improvement on our luck to date. Andrew thought long and hard and depending on the weather the next day, he said that we may move camp and head back towards Arctic Bay. We were all very tired and quickly drank our hot chocolate. I for one could have fallen sound asleep while I was sitting down. Qamayuq got up and left to go to his own tent, and we bedded down in our sleeping bags. I lay there thinking about the wonderful day I had just had, sixteen hours of uninterrupted, vibrant excitement and the best single experience that I have ever had in my life, who could ask for more?

By the time I fell asleep, I had not even reached ice cube mountain on the outbound journey and I think Roland and Andrew had fallen asleep just as quick. We had only been asleep for an hour or so when Andrew sprung out of his sleeping bag like a jack-in-a-box with an overcharged spring. Which brought Roland and myself out of our sleeping mode with immediate effect. As I opened my eyes, he was already unzipping the tent and calling me to come and take a look. I had not a clue what was going on or why he had reacted so fast.

He had been awakened by the howl of the dogs. They were calling in a very unusual way. Even I could detect sheer panic in their voices, they were screaming for their lives. Andrew moved aside to let me look, as he continued to unzip the tent. It was total disbelief, I stood looking in amazement and horror as a polar bear walked up and down the line of dogs deciding which one he wanted to eat for breakfast. We watched helplessly not daring to draw attention to ourselves in case it decided to charge us as Andrew's rifle was on the snowmobile. It is difficult to describe just how disturbed the dogs were. They were each on a short leash tied to the chain. Some were running around in circles, others were jumping side to side, and most of the remainder were standing, with their tales outstretched, hair on end, and their ears up and pointing forwards, and all of them were barking with a terrified vicious face and showing their teeth. They were trying to look as big and vicious as possible to scare off the bear, meanwhile the bear was undeterred and was challenging one of the dogs which had set its teeth and was jumping towards the bear. I don't know why it was hesitating, it could have killed the dog with one sweep of its paw.

We had no choice but to start shouting and waving our hands at the bear. It looked up at us, but it clearly was not interested at all. It was thinking about its dinner. Andrew ran outside dressed only in his underpants to get his rifle from the snowmobile. He picked it up, this is the one that I had previously described, the one that was bound together with electrical tape with no sites and a rusty barrel, and let off a warning shot to try to scare the bear away, but the bullet hit it in the back leg. It jumped up and moved three yards away from the dogs, an injured bear is even more dangerous. Qamayuq had come out of his tent and was standing shivering beside us. They quickly exchanged words. He is

on the wildlife committee for Arctic Bay and the surrounding area, and although I could not interpret what they were saying word for word, I knew the gist of what they were saying, they had got to finish it off. There was no alternative, you could not leave an injured bear to have a long, slow death.

Andrew took a second shot which hit it but again did not kill it, and it started to run off dragging its back leg. He ran after the bear still dressed only in his vest and underpants and without any boots. I heard two further shots and then he returned to the tent. He was absolutely freezing, his hands shaking and shrugging his shoulders to try to warm up. Once he was inside, I rubbed his feet between my hands to warm them up and restore the circulation while Roland lit the stove and then chopped up some ice to boil and make a hot drink. With the stove glowing on full heat and the tent zipped down, it soon began to warm up. I pulled out my sixty-year-old bottle of Glen Moray single malt and poured a couple of drams into each of the mugs of coffee which warmed all of us from inside to outside. This was done not so much to celebrate the killing of the bear but for medicinal purposes only, hence it was added to the coffee which otherwise would have been a sacrilege to drink it that way. Roland enjoyed it, but the two old partners did not comment and drank it anyway.

Once Andrew was warmed up, he got dressed and went with Qamayuq to bring back the bear with the snowmobile. It was a young female about four years old. It was such a shame no one would have knowingly wanted to shoot a female, but this one could not be avoided. The pair of them set to and started skinning it. You could clearly see that they had done this job before. They were so fast that you would have thought that it was buttoned up or had a zip. When it came to skin the head, Andrew took control. If you make a mistake on this, the value of the skin drops in half. He carefully skinned out the ears, muzzle, and around the eyes, while Qamayuq started on the paws.

I was intrigued and didn't stop watching for a second. Although I had skinned a lot of animals myself, I was still learning and I knew that by watching a professional, it would improve and fine tune my skills. Once the skin was removed, they stretched it out on the ice and folded it hair to hair and then rolled it up.

The next job was to eviscerate it, but we gave it a close examination to see where it had been hit, apart from the first bullet which hit the leg. The other shots hit the vital organs. It really was miraculous that it managed to go over a hundred yards before it eventually collapsed. It must have been moving on pure adrenaline to get so far. When they opened it up, the thoracic cavity was totally filled with blood and most of the liver was liquidized to a thick mush.

I knew what we were going to have for dinner that night, and I was looking forward to eating my first polar bear steak. If it tasted as good as the black bear which I ate in Alaska, then it really would be a gastronomic delight, but for now we all wanted to go back to bed. When I awoke, I decided to take my last stroll around the iceberg and then I came back to write up my log. I started by saying that it had been a fantastic day, we didn't shoot the polar bear in the way I had expected by finding it and then stalking it to get in range but nonetheless we had bagged a white bear to add to my collection. There wouldn't be too many hunters

who had a black, brown, and white bear in their trophy room. I wrote that it did not even matter to me that I didn't pull the trigger of the gun which killed the bear, the whole experience of living on the ice, eating, drinking, and working with three truly professional hunters, whose whole life and livelihood revolves around hunting subsistence and not for trophies like myself and scores of other hunters who go out hunting for sport. Hunting to the Inuit is essential to keep the wolf from the door and feed their families. I had learnt about their culture, history, and how the white man had changed their lives, which in many ways was not for the better. We always seem to think that by introducing aboriginals, from any part of the world where we find them, to our capitalistic lifestyle that we have improved their lot, but in reality, we have intruded into their lives and introduced them to new social pressures to cope with, which before our two cultures met did not exist. We view this as an improvement to the quality of their lives, but in many instances, it is far from the truth. Obesity and depression are two examples, which are a growing part of our society, and I have noticed that they are also creeping into aboriginal communities in many parts of the world caused by stress and unhealthy living and nutrition.

Hunting in the Arctic was never on my shopping list. It was sudden and totally unexpected, and if I had never rang Joe to check up on my moose hunt in the fall, then it would never ever have happened; therefore, I felt that this hunt was a chance of fate and meant to be. Without doubt, this was the best hunting experience that I had ever had and I couldn't imagine that any hunt that I would do in the future would not be able to become a close second. This stood alone on a mountain of ice cubes.

Living out on the ice for over three weeks with Andrew, Roland, and Qamayuq was remarkable. For the first two days, they saw me and looked after me as they would any other hunting clientele who was paying them for their services, but things changed very rapidly and permanently. We were quickly working as a team, and we had become true friends. I dosed off while I was writing, and I think that they must have felt sorry for me as they left me until the dinner was ready. This time, the cooking smells didn't arouse me, so I must have been darn well tired, but when I did awaken, the smell made my mouth water. It goes without saying that the bear was divine and all four of us went back for a second helping. From being on the breadline, we now had meat in abundance and we had enough to give the dogs a rare treat too, that's if Andrew would allow them an extra portion.

After dinner, I laid back and tried to play my mouth organ. I can't put two notes together and my dad had been trying to teach me, but it is as bad as trying to teach a soldier to march who has two left feet. My intentions are good, but I feel a right dude because I would love to learn an instrument, as I am as passionate about music, as I am about hunting and not being able to string two notes together makes me feel really inadequate. I cannot even play a little tune on a penny whistle. I was struggling away when Andrew popped his head into the tent and told me to put my boots on as we were leaving in a few minutes. 'Leaving where?'

'To find your polar bear, of course.'

'But we've got the bear.'

'No, no, I had to kill that one because it was going to kill one of my dogs. I know it was an accident and I really only wanted to scare it, but out here in the wilderness, you are allowed to kill a bear in self-defence or if it is attacking another person or in the defence of your dogs which are our means of transport. Not every Inuit has a snowmobile, but we all have dogs.'

This took me totally by surprise. In my mind, the hunt was over; we had our polar bear lying on the sledge.

Andrew wanted one last look around ice cube mountain. He was positive that there was a male in that area. It was only a matter of luck. Sooner or later our paths would cross, and he was giving it one last chance before we moved camp and headed back home in the morning. Stunned as I was, I did as I was told and put my boots on, picked up my rifle, and went to help Andrew. As always, they gave us their recital and bounced with happiness as I untied them from the chain and led them to Andrew to harness them onto the sledge.

We went off by ourselves as he had left the other guys to dismantle the boat and return it to the dog kennel as would be needing it the next day when we headed back to Arctic Bay. They gave us a big wave, and Roland shouted, 'Good luck! I've got a feeling that he will be there waiting for you'. I hope he was right, but deep down I felt that the polar bear was going to be the winner this time. You can work as hard as you can and glass for twenty-four hours a day, but you need a bit of luck to let your paths cross and only then does your skill as a hunter or stalker and your ability to shoot straight, under stressful conditions, come into play.

This was probably my last chance to enjoy riding on the dog sledge, and I was determined to lap up every last minute, it was a true adventure, exciting with all the thrills of riding any fast machine. The previous day's snowfall had covered our tracks which didn't bother Andrew too much as he had his own built in GPS and knew exactly where he was going. But what it did do was to allow us to identify any fresh tracks which had arrived since the storm and we weren't long before we saw some. Four bears had come out of the ice cube terrain and were heading inland towards the mountains. The first spoors that we found was once again a mother bear with three cubs which is rather unusual as most bears normally have twins. Andrew said that they were moving very quickly and they looked very, very fresh, so he decided by pure instinct to follow them for a while and see what would come of it. This proved very lucrative because after half an hour, another set of tracks joined them and this time it was one of those big males and a very big male at that.

We had spent day after day and hour upon hour without success scanning the brilliant white snow and ice looking for our bear and here just by chance we were on to a fresh trail of a big male. I just couldn't believe our luck. Andrew said that it must be fairly close because the dogs could smell it and they were not going to stop until they had caught it up. For the umpteenth time adrenalin was starting to pump my blood fast around my body and I was becoming more and more excited. I was nearly wetting myself, which is not the best thing to do in my present situation. Remember none of us had even washed ourselves for three weeks. I had lost all my composure. The thought of seeing that illusive big male whose absence had eluded us each day was blowing my mind out of control. Now it would be our turn to be lucky and the last laugh would be on us.

The dogs were running as fast as they could without any encouragement from Andrew, and more to the point, any world-class skier would have been proud of my performance, I was riding the sledge like a true master, balancing and counter-balancing and distributing my weight as though it was second nature and keeping the sledge firmly on its course, it was such a thrilling experience that the excitement was overwhelming, so much so that I had actually had forgotten about the polar bear as the ride was so much fun by itself.

Andrew shouted at the dogs and told them to slow down and then to stop. Then he took out his telescope and his tripod. He had spotted something well into the distance. I looked firstly with my naked eye and then with binoculars but could not find the bear. He then let me look through his scope and it was still difficult, but I eventually saw a single bear which he said was a male. How he spotted it I just don't know, seeing white on white at that distance is incredible! He must have the eyes better than those of a hawk. Now that we had found it, what was the plan of attack? At the moment, it was so far ahead that we should follow it as fast as the dogs can run, so he cracked his whip and we were off once again. We were slowly catching it up, but this could go on for hours, if the bear didn't stop, and Andrew did not think it would, as it was following the female with her cubs. She was either giving out signs that she was on heat or he wanted to kill the cubs, which is not as common in polar bears as it is in other species like lions and tigers, but the latter might be the reason. Anyhow for the present time, our strategy was that we would try to catch him up and reduce the ground between us. Believe me I still wanted to shoot a bear, but at this moment in time, it was not as important as it was earlier in the day before Andrew had shot the young female. I had had my climax. I was thrilled with the success of our hunt.

I don't know what it is like on a bobsleigh whizzing down a mountain and balancing as your sleigh hits a bend, but I would imagine that every nerve in your body is on tenterhooks. Your head is in a spin and you are enjoying every minute even though your brain realises that you are in a dangerous situation, all be it hopefully in a controlled one. Cross these feelings with those you get when skiing very fast down a steep slope and you are now, as close to how I feel at this very moment. My mind was definitely not focused on hunting a polar bear.

Andrew looked back over his shoulder and told me that we were catching it up and we would eventually get there and win. He was still doing everything he could to get me the king of the Arctic, and so long as the dogs kept going, he would continue to. Sheer perseverance and the desire to succeed drove him on and on. He certainly was not a man who would throw in the towel and give up without a fight. An attitude like this stems from the necessity to do anything and everything to survive in such adverse conditions that makes you appreciate just how lucky we are. This and similar unpleasant and harsh conditions in other parts of the world make me wonder why they continue to live in this way especially when they, through the media, particularly television, can see that there is an easier world outside your present existence.

We continued on regardless, in pursuit of the bear and it looked like our luck was in this time as the bear had stopped, hopefully it was for a good rest as it had been travelling at some pace. We started to gain ground quite quickly. It had actually decided to lie down and either didn't notice our presence or did not see us as a threat and allowed us to come within 500 yards of it. Andrew stopped the dogs and then took out his telescope to check it out. The bear was lying broadside on with its head quietly resting between its paws. My heart was pounding on my ribs and my nerves were on edge and fighting each other. We only had to make it another 250 yards and the bear was as good as dead.

I removed my rifle from its sleeve and picked up my bipod. We crouched as low to the snow as we could and moved forwards towards the bear, leaving the dogs behind and keeping one eye on it all the time so that we could stop instantly if it looked towards us. We knew that what wind there was would be working in our favour and the only way it would be aware of our presence was if it saw us move, so we crept slowly towards it on our knees. Suddenly the bear stood up and did a 180-degree turn and then it laid down again. We both looked through our binoculars and I checked the distance on my built in range finder; it was reading at 363 yards. It was well within my range, but after seeing how hard our last bear was to kill, I preferred to be down to 250, to know that I could kill it cleanly.

I gave Andrew the thumbs up and was about to tell him that I wanted to crawl closer, but when I looked at him, his face was unreal. He looked shocked, scared, and nervous. Alarm bells began to ring. Something was seriously wrong and I needed to find out what the problem was and find it out now. He looked at me straight in the face and all he could say was, 'No kill. No kill. Please, no kill, Dave.'

I was at a complete loss to understand why he did not want me to kill this bear. We had been hunting for a male polar bear for over two weeks and glassing eighteen hours a day and sometimes more. Now that we had one within our grasp and I was only seconds away from killing it, he did not want me to shoot it. All he could do was to ask me to look at its face. He was working himself up into a state of frenzy. He looked white with fright and was very, very upset and I still had not worked out why. We had disturbed the bear and it looked straight at me. I then had a full view of its face and saw that it had a massive scar on its muzzle from the left ear down to the tip of its nose. We could not see this when it was lying the other way around. Andrew had recognised it immediately when it turned around and I then knew why he did not want me to shoot it, he had recognised the bear, but the question was why did he not want it shot. The only reason that I could think of was that he must have had a previous important experience with this bear and that was why he did not want me to kill it.

He was so upset that he was unable to tell me, and I knew that I would have to wait for the answer until we were back in camp where Roland could give me the explanation. For now, all he was able to say was 'no kill, thank you, no kill, thank you, Dave'. If it had been another hunter and this had happened, it could have caused an explosion and a big one at that, they, like me, would have paid an arm and a leg for a polar bear hunt and to abort it when one was about to pull the trigger would be a crisis of vast proportions.

Believe me, I was quite relaxed about it. I had so much respect for Andrew that if he did not want me to shoot the bear, there must be a very good reason. We had become such good friends that all I wanted to do was to relieve his stress.I emtied the shells from my rifle and I tried to indicate to him that there was no problem and when he realised this, he started to settle down. I saw him take a few deep breaths and then he patted me on my back and said, 'Thank you'. This was in no way going to spoil our hunting expedition.

We sat there on the sledge and continued to watch his bear watching us until he finally decided he had had enough. He turned swiftly and got on with his own business, chasing after the female. For our part, we decided to retrace our tracks and head back to camp, rather to continue on to ice cube mountain. Andrew was not in a hurry and went pretty easy on the dogs as they had worked exceptionally hard following the bear, that wasn't to be. It was another enthralling journey and now my riding skills were second nature I had time to think, without worrying whether or not I was going to fall of the sledge. Why did he not want me to shoot 'Scarface'? There must be a very strong reason and I couldn't wait to find out.

When we arrived back at camp, the dog kennel was as good as new and back on Andrew's sledge, both tents were packed away and the polar bear meat which was frozen solid was tied on my sledge just in front of my cabin. All that was left out was the stove with a boiling pan of water ready to make us a hot drink.

Andrew went straight to Roland to ask him to explain to me why he had asked me not to shoot Scarface which will forever be its name. Roland was astonished that we had passed over this bear; unfortunately, it was the only one that we had seen throughout the whole hunt and we both were happy to let it live another day. They didn't know how or where to start but began by telling me that Scareface was five years old and he was now in his prime but the reason that they knew this was the start of the story. Andrew had saved his life as a cub when he was out hunting five years ago. He saw a big male bear attack it. With its front paw, he flung it into the air and in doing so its claw had caught the cub's face and has slashed open its muzzle. It was lying there quite helpless. Andrew fired some warning shot into the air and scared off the male bear. The mother had already moved out of the way to protect her other cub. He then went to look at the baby cub and found that it was still very much alive and he then decided to stitch the wound on its face which they did quite successfully. It was full of joy and was bouncing around showing no signs that it had been assaulted by the male, so then they followed the mother's tracks and repatriated it. The mother was glad to see her cub again and immediately started to lick the cub's wound. This was a very good start. They watched her for a while and then left her and her cubs to their own devises and to fend for themselves in the wilderness. Andrew did not see him the following year but caught up with him the year after and now he had seen him again with me. I fully appreciated his feelings for the bear. I myself once found a young fawn with a broken leg on my estate. I strapped it up and it too did survive and went on to have her own fawns. I called her 'hopalong' and she had my protection for the rest of her life.

I told Roland that I wasn't really bothered, I had got the polar bear's pelt which Andrew had shot, and although it was a lot smaller than the skin of Scarface, it would make a good rug. It was then that he explained that I could not have the bear's skin as she was a female and would be confiscated by the Fish and Wildlife department when we arrived back in Arctic Bay. Had it been a male, we could have counted it as my trophy, but it wasn't a male.

When you present your skin to the wildlife officer, you also have to give him both the skull and the penis. I did not know this and it put the passing over of Scarface in a different complexion, but I have absolutely no regrets for not taking the opportunity to shoot my polar bear and as a result I was going home empty-handed. This thought passed in and out of my brain in seconds, as even if I had known that the bear skin was going to be confiscated, I still would not have shot Scarface. He was much too precious to Andrew and sometimes, 'whatever will be, will be', even if things do not work out the way you would have liked them to.

You might find the mentality of most hunters is difficult to understand. We all have a deep love of animals and nature. At times we go out of our way to help them out of some trouble, yet at other times seek to kill them. To be a good hunter, you need to understand your quarry, you need to know their habits, when they eat, what they eat, and all their daily routines and have a deep passion and love of nature.

We packed the stove and then headed away from iceberg camp for the last time. Even if I came back next year, the features would not be the same. I sat on my sledge looking back at iceberg camp until it totally disappeared from view. I had a deep feeling of sadness more than I had ever felt before when I have finished a hunt. Every day there was simply awesome, the spirit of the ice was buried deep inside me and I knew that I would take it with me to my grave.

As my final images of iceberg camp blurred into the horizon, I turned around to see where we were heading. The mountains were still not in view and we had already been travelling for some hours. I had been nibbling away at my almonds and chewing my last kumquats. I was now rationing them out. It's like eating a fresh fruit lolly, and they are simply delicious.

I felt very sorry for the dogs. They had already done a day's work before we set off from iceberg camp, how much more would Andrew ask of them? I've never before seen any animals with such stamina. It is totally unbelievable how they perform on such little food.

As the sight of the mountains gradually came into view, I noticed that Andrew was no longer moving towards them but was steering a path parallel to them, and when we stopped for a hot chocolate, I asked him what his plan was. He said that he wanted to take us for about another hour and then make camp. This was where the other guys had found fresh prints the previous day. We could not go too far as we were running out of fuel, but we could explore the area the next day and if necessary possibly the day after. If we did so, it would mean that we would have to drive the last stage continuously, only stopping to eat and not making a final camp at iglu camp as we did coming. Oh my god! This will be a hell of a journey and not one that I would not relish or be looking forward to. It would be hard for me but even harder for them.

We never came any closer to the mountains as we followed the boundary between the pack ice and the ice cube terrain which stretched out as far as the eyes could see. We stopped to set up camp. We did so as though it was a permanent camp and not a one-night stand. Andrew was going to give it his best shot which he had already said might mean making a continuous final leg.

Once I had helped Roland to erect our tent, I went across to help move the dogs out of the kennel and onto the chain. For the first and the only time, they made a petted whimper and missed out the spectacular chorus which they had sang on every previous occasion. They must have been well and truly knackered and I can't blame them, they worked harder than a team of Irish navies and they can take some beating,believe me.

Now that we had them all tied to the chain, we started to feed them. Under Andrew's close supervision, I chopped up the forequarters of the bear into joints of the required size which Andrew subsequently fed to each dog. We too were also having polar bear for dinner which was a welcome treat after the longest day that we have had spent on the ice to date. I skipped the coffee and dived straight into my sleeping bag, pulled the cords around the hood, and was dead to the world in milliseconds.

From what Roland had told me in the morning, he spent half an hour chatting with his dad about 'Scarface', seemingly his dad was saying that he wished that he had not asked me not to kill it. We all had worked very long hours to get close to a male bear and it was for his own personal reasons that he did not want it shot. He felt even worse because I had granted his wishes so amicably and without any disagreement and showed no signs of even being upset over the incident. He said that he felt guilty and a right heal and truly regretted everything and that he had a skin at home in his freezer that he would give me as a trophy.

I asked Roland to tell his father that it was not a problem to me whatsoever, and I had no regrets about not shooting Scarface. I was pleased that he showed so much compassion to help the young injured cub in the first place. I was so pleased that I could do something to please his dad as he had worked so hard and tried so hard to please me. So that is the end of the matter and I did not want to hear anymore about it.

After breakfast of pancakes and crispy bacon with maple syrup yet again, this may sound boring, but I never got sick of it, Andrew came and gave me a big hug and said come on let's go and get your bear. I knew that everything was ready to go as I had heard the dog's chorus when Andrew and Qamayuq were harnessing the dogs to their sledge. They were in good fettle after a well-earned rest and a meal. The lead dog appeared to bark to the others as we threw our last dice and were off. I was still as optimistic as ever. You become that way when you are hunting and fishing. You have the same odds today as you had yesterday, we only needed our paths to cross and we were in business. After we had been away for an hour, we heard Roland and Qamayuq following our tracks. This time they were both on the same snowmobile as they were trying to conserve fuel which made me a little nervous at the time, but I soon forgot all about it and concentrated on looking out for a bear.

When they caught us up, we stopped for a coffee, and Andrew climbed onto the top of a group of ice cubes to scan. We had not even finished drinking our coffee when Andrew shouted to tell us that he could see a big bear and most importantly it was coming in our direction. We all climbed up beside him and he pointed out the animal. It was still out on the furtherest range of my binoculars, but he said that it sure was cruising on. The trouble was that first you could see it and then it disappeared behind a group of ice cubes; some minutes later, it reappeared and then it was lost again. After watching it for a while, Andrew decided that we should move further down on the dog sledge. It was just as well that they had been rested and fed as the poor buggers had now to pull four men as he did not want to take a chance that it might be scared off by the sound of the snowmobile. He stopped every 200 or 300 yards to check where it was and when he was happy and had found it, we moved on a bit further.

We followed this procedure for quite a distance until Andrew decided that we were close to where we needed to be and that we should continue on foot. I crept up to look over a large ice cube to see where it was and I got a very quick sighting before it vanished again. This was it. This was going to be my last chance to shoot my polar bear, with or without a facial scar. Andrew checked it over. It was a fantastic bear and he left the others behind and chose a good position for me to take my shot. He told me to kneel down between two ice cubes and he placed his jacket on the one in front for my rest. I loaded a round into the chamber and waited. If the bear continued on its projected path, it would come in range at around 150 yards away in about three or four minutes. The pressure was intense. My heart was beating ten to the minute and my stomach was whirling around like a washing machine with a brick inside. I tried looking through my scope, but I could not hold the rifle still. 'Come on, Dave, you have made plenty of kills before, stop being stupid.' Andrew could see that I was very nervous and patted me on the shoulder and told me to take a deep breath. I did one, I did two, and on the third, the bear came full broadside into my sights.

He was simply spectacular. He knew that we were there and turned his head sideways to have a good, long look at his executioner. For the first time in a half century of hunting, that is exactly how I felt. An executioner. *Not*, a hunter who had worked very, very hard with his guides and had reached that final point of killing his quarry, but simply an executioner. I was about to take the life of a magnificent creature and rather than it being an exhilarating experience and a moment of my life that I had looked forwards to, it was giving me no pleasure at all and was making me feel as sick as a pig or somewhat even worse than that. Andrew whispered in my ear and told me he is ready to shoot, shoot now. I still hesitated and my mind went back to the previous day with Scarface. If Andrew had not asked me not to kill him I know that I would have pulled the trigger then, without any further consideration.

But now I was in an entirely different scenario. The situation was very different, or I felt that it was. His eyes were passionate and were appealing to my inner feelings. I had a massive sense of guilt which was so strong, even before I had done anything to be guilty of. Everything was telling me to let it pass.

Andrew whispered into my ear once more, 'Dave, shoot him now, or he will move on, what's the problem?' He was not in a hurry to go anywhere. He stood perfectly still in that unique pose which only polar bears have. It is shaped like a wedge, the highest part being the top of his back at the rear end, then sloping gently down towards to his head. Take this broadside image and turn his head through ninety degrees so that his head is looking straight at you. If you add in those appealing eyes, you will have a clear picture of what was confronting me through my scope. Andrew gave me a little poke and repeated his words, 'Shoot it now, Dave'.

I turned my head and looked up at him in a most sympathetic and appealing manner asking for Andrew not to press me any further and hoping that when I looked back, he might have moved away and would have avoided me having to make one of the hardest decision in my hunting life. I looked again, and he hadn't moved even an eyelid. It was my call and I had to make it pretty soon or he would eventually continue on his way. Oh, if only I could let him pass! My mind cast back to all the long hours we spent day after day at temperatures well below minus thirty and looking for a male polar bear and now I had one in my rifle sights, how, how in the name of God was I going to explain to those three Inuit hunters that after all we had endured to find a bear, when push comes to shove, I did not have the balls to carry it through and kill it.

Andrew knew that there was something wrong and that I had a problem just as I knew that he had one the previous day, and he was about to make my decision for me. He stood up and the bear looked at him. In an instant, I looked directly through my scope, put the cross hairs on its heart clearly avoiding to take one last look in its face, and gently squeezed the trigger as I had done so many times before. We both heard the deep thud as the bear slumped to the ice. Andrew congratulated me and told me to give it another bullet, but I told him that there was no need to, the bear was dead. David had slain his giant of the ice, but David came close to vomiting. I felt sad and wasn't proud of my actions. 'et tu Brutus.' It evoked a sense of desolate emptiness. I stood alone and cried.

I didn't feel elated. I wasn't even pleased with my performance of killing it with one single bullet through the heart although I was pleased that it did not suffer the pain of death as other animals often do. I felt very guilty and ashamed that I had killed it because I did not have the guts to tell Andrew and the others that I did not have the heart to shoot. After all I had passed over one the previous day to help Andrew. This was my decision and mine alone, and it was wrong for me to try to put any blame for my actions at their feet. The one thing that I did decide was that polar bear did not die in vain. I committed myself there and then, even before we walked to the stricken polar bear or took any photographs, that I was going to write a book on this adventure and all the profits to the last penny would be given to a charity to help save the Polar Bears in the Arctic. That is how and why,my book *The Arctic, the Inuit, and the Polar Bear* was conceived.

I knew that I could do it because I had many years ago had written some articles and had them published in a shooting magazines, and at that time, they asked me to write more, but I never got around to writing them. This time I had the best reason in the world to write, to raise funds to support the polar bear, all that I had to do was to discipline myself and make the time available to accomplish it.

Roland was soon on the scene, and having heard only one shot, their first question they asked Andrew was 'Did Dave kill it?' We all went across to see the bear. It lay there with its brilliant white hair shining in the sunlight, spoiled only by its cherry red blood dripping from the wound onto the clean white snow. Their excitement was unbelievable. I could see the relief on their faces as we hugged and danced together in celebration of our success. Everyone had worked so hard and we kept ourselves motivated to the very last day even when we knew that time was clearly not on our side and none of us wanted to return to Arctic Bay without one.

We all walked over to inspect the bear and the funeral ritual then began. They started to lay the bear out in a good position for taking some photographs. Roland programmed his camera into the delay mode so all of us could be on the photograph. This was the most important

photograph for all of us. We had made a great team and now we had a permanent record of the occasion that we all could cherish even when it was just a memory. When the ceremony was over, I stood there looking down on my trophy and wishing that I'd stayed in bed and today was still a dream, meanwhile Roland walked back to fetch the snowmobile so that we could use its power to pull the bear out of the ice cube terrain and onto to the flat ice where we could dress it out.

Once again I looked at Andrew and I could see the relief on Andrew's face. The anxiety had vanished and he started at last to relax. He had achieved exactly what he had set out to do even though it was a close call. Now we did not have to drive the last leg without a break, which we all were prepared to do, in order to get that extra day's hunting had it proved necessary. This day's hunt made us all feel very happy, life is life, blood is blood and dead is dead, and there was no going back. It was me and only me who made the decision to shoot it.

Now that we had pulled the bear out onto the sea ice and ready for skinning and we knew that we would not be camping this side of the mountain, so Andrew sent Roland and Qamayuq back to pick up the dogs and then to go back to camp and start dismantling it, put the dog's sleigh on Qamayuq's sledge and then the dogs back into their kennel. This would save us a lot of time and get us as far as we could through the mountains before we had to make camp. Once they finished that work, one of them could return for us and hopefully we would have finished preparing the bear. I had already decided to use all my resources to write a book to raise money to help protect the Arctic polar bears from extinction, but I also decided to have a full mount made of my emperor of the Arctic. He was much too precious and the platinum medal of my trophies to be turned into a rug as I had done with my brown and black bears. He had sacrificed his life and I felt that I owed him that at the very least.

Andrew was happy to let me help at least with the preliminary work. Once we reached the paws, I watched him skin out his paw and then he kept a good eye on me while I was skinning mine. This bear had taken a lot of finding and he was not going to let me mess it up in any way. He gave me a smile and a nod of approval which is a great complement from a professional hunter which he was. I started on the hind feet while he did the delicate work and skinned out the head. If you make a mistake here, it will totally ruin a trophy especially if you are going to have it as a full mount which I had decided to do.

We had just finished the skinning when we heard the snowmobile approaching. Roland had left Qamayuq to put the dogs back into the kennel. They had finished their hard work on this hunt and were entitled to an easy ride back to Arctic Bay.

We then set about butchering the carcass by first removing the shoulders and then the hind legs right up to the pelvis. We removed the strip loins and loaded the meat onto the front of my sledge. Being an old bear, that is all the meat that they were going to take and were leaving the rest to be cannibalised by other bears. I said that I would like the fillets as they would be the most tender part of the beast. They did not really understand what I wanted and I could not explain it any better. So I rolled up my sleeves and drew my knife across its abdomen exposing the abdominal cavity that was filled with blood. Gripping my knife, I plunged in my hand and cut the intestine where it comes out of the diaphragm and then proceeded to eviscerate it. Andrew and Roland stood there gobsmacked once more. They had never ever seen a hunter even touching a bear. All of them leave this work to the guides. They saw that I was struggling to turn the bear over to drain it and pull out the entrails so they came to help. I was then able to quickly remove both fillets, wash down my arms with snow, and the job was done.

It only took minutes to reach Qamayuq and we now started the long track back to Arctic Bay. To all intents and purposes, my Arctic expedition was over. I can't help but repeat this, but it was a truly and totally unexpected part of my life that I will never ever

forget. It had only been seven weeks from the first time the idea was mooted by Joe as a possible hunt and now it was all over. I never really got much time to think and get excited about the prospect of going deep inside the Arctic Circle and living with the Inuits, but I will have plenty of time, in fact the rest of my life to lament over this once in a lifetime event.

The serious business now was to get back home. It took us five hours to drive to the foot of the mountain pass and I was on my last rations of almonds and kumquats which had been an excellent antidote to relive my body from the cold conditions. From there we had at least a minimum of a twenty-hour drive ahead of us. As I stood up holding onto the rope around the cabin, my mood was flat and pensive and I looked back at the frozen sea for one last time before we reached the summit and then started the long decent down to iglu camp. I wondered whether it had withstood the storms and was waiting to provide me with another night's shelter or if I would have my last night in the Arctic wilderness in Andrew's tent. Either way it would be my last night and that made me very sad, but it is inevitable that all good things have to come to an end. The next day will be a new day on the horizon and only God knows what that will bring. I felt grateful and honoured that they had taken me into their hearts and made me part of their family. Deep inside, I knew that I would be back one day. I would love to see the Arctic in the summer and go fishing for Arctic charr and hunting for caribou and narwhal, and for learning to carve a polar bear in stone. I did have that to look forward to when I got back to Arctic Bay. I had done a deal with Peter. He said that he would teach me the basic principles when we returned. I did have three more nights in the village before I had to leave for Ottawa and I was going to make the most of them.

Qamayuq had taken the lead of our party through the mountains followed by Roland and me, with Andrew bringing up the tail. He must have been homesick as he was belting on and creating a snowstorm, and my new skill of riding a sledge was improving all the time. My knees were acting as springs and absorbing the shock waves as the sledge hit hidden ridges of ice. I spotted a beautiful ice carving made from icicles, around what in summer would be a waterfall and tried to get the attention of Roland to get him to stop so that I could take a picture. He could not hear me shouting and it took a lucky throw of one of my last frozen kumquats to hit him on the back before he looked around to see what I wanted. Qamayuq was still going like the clappers, but when I looked around to show him the icicles, Andrew was nowhere to be seen. We now had a major problem, Qamayuq was virtually out of sight and we had to retrace our tracks to find out what had happened to Andrew. We just had to hope that sooner or later Qamayuq would look around and find that we were both missing and retrace his steps and come back to look for us.

Andrew was well over a mile away and when we reached him, he already had released the dog sledge and his new snowmobile was on its side. He was frantically trying to remove the covers for the engine to diagnose the problem. Unfortunately, like myself he was no mechanic. This was Qamayuq's job and he was bloody miles away. What made matters worse was that he had all the tools with him and we had no alternative but to wait until he realised that we were no longer following him and he came back to look for us. We were simply helpless and powerless. The ball was firmly in his court and we could not do anything about it. The minutes seemed to be hours. You know how it is when you are waiting for a train which is running late. You know that it is eventually going to come, but you don't know when and time doesn't half drag.

I really felt sorry for Andrew. He had been under a lot of stress as the hunt proved to be a very difficult one, and when he was starting to relax, this hit him full whack in the chest. Life is a sod at times but as they say, it all goes with the territory, and I'm sure that he had been in worse situations in the past and whatever the outcome, he would take this in his stride, even if it had made us a lot more work. The silence was eventually broken by the sound of Qamayuq's snowmobile. We could hear it before we could see it as the sound waves were channelled through the valley, but it was only a matter of minutes before he came into sight. Oh boy, we were relieved to see him, but we weren't out of the woods yet. Qamayuq was very apologetic and immediately started to strip down the snowmobile. Once the covers were off, the problem was exposed and we didn't like what we saw, the main cog on the drive shaft for some reason had shattered. It looked like we would have to abandon it, drive back to Arctic Bay where hopefully we could find a spare, and come back to fix it. This was a new machine and still under guarantee and had only done a few days' work before we set out on our hunt, but new or not the cog was broken and the reality of the situation was that we were stuck in the mountains and hours away from Arctic Bay, without any means of fixing it.

I don't know what inspired Qamayuq to remove all the tools that were kept under his seat. I think he went to find an Allen key, but when he did, he came across a similar cog in the bottom of his tool box. This was years old and had been there for ages. It was not even a replacement for his own machine and he did not know why it was still there but it was and it would be worth a try and might get us out of our difficulty. The cog was held in place by some type of sliding bush which took a lot of persuading to release its grip, but when it did, we were able to remove the broken one and replace it with the one Qamayuq had found. As luck would have it and when you throw shit some of it always sticks, it fitted and we all sighed with relief. This hunt was not going to reveal all its secrets until the very end. The only difference was that the groove for the drive belt was not the same size. This was better than nothing and hopefully it would last long enough to get us home. It was soon back in working order and we were again back on the trail heading for home, but Andrew was back as the leader of the pack.

Overall, we had lost a couple of hours because of the breakdown and now a storm was brewing up which made me pleased that Andrew was now guiding us, and this time, he was not going to turn back as we were over the worst part of the mountains and he was able to find his way, even when the visibility was down to a couple of hundred yards.

The problem with my new travelling position was that my face was exposed to the elements and you had the wind chill effect in addition to the cold temperature. I held the rope with one hand and used the other to cover my face below my goggles. This was still a lot better than sitting inside the cabin and being hit with the vibrations of every bump.

When we eventually reached iglu camp, I was in for a big surprise. There were two snowmobiles parked by my iglu, and as we approached, two men crawled out of it to greet us. That answered one question, the iglu had withstood the storms. One of the men was another of Andrew's sons and the other was his friend who had come out to keep him company and as a buddy because they never travel alone, it's much too dangerous to travel alone. Andrew had contacted them by satellite phone to ask them to bring out some more fuel, the situation had been more critical than he had let on. They had also brought us a present, two large thermos flasks filled with hot soup which went down a treat. After twenty days, it was nice to see a new face, especially one who brought us two flasks of soup and some fuel to get us home.

Andrew came across to see me. He said that he did not know how bad the storm was going to be, but the lads had said that when they heard the forecast in Arctic Bay, it was expected to last for a few days and that it would be safer to keep going. If I had no objection, this is what he would prefer to do. I was more than happy with Andrew's decisions whatever he decides to do. This one especially, as it would give me more time to spend in the village, an extra night in the comfort of a proper bed, and most importantly, the luxury of a soak in a hot bath, earlier than I had expected. In any case once you are heading for home as we were now, you have a different mindset altogether.

That was the end of my romantic night sleeping in the iglu, but I knew that it would be better to get home in one piece than face any unknown and maybe catastrophic problems with bad weather. I had the easy job, but how about the rest of the gang, they had already driven for hours? Were they happy to continue? It was thumbs up, and they too wanted to head for home.

If we had not shot the bear, then we had already decided that we would camp for an extra day and drive the last leg without a stop, so what was the difference now. We were doing it out as a choice. He said that now we have enough fuel, we can now drive at full throttle as unknown to me they had been taking it easy to conserve fuel.

What we have to do now is to let the dogs out of the kennel for a quick walk and a pee as they must be pretty desperate to cock their legs, and in order to keep them under control, they had to be released in twos and threes, otherwise, we might have a massive dog fight on our hands. In some ways, these Inuit dogs have a fairly primitive attitude and the instinct to survive at all costs is as strong in them as it is in their master's. Everyone helped in this massive dog pissing session and we soon had them back in their kennel and tied up for the remainder of the journey.

The snowstorm had eased slightly while we were drinking our soup and walking the dogs, and Andrew wanted to be away while the going was good. You still could not see more than 150 yards ahead and these guys were pushing ahead with their foot fully down on the throttle. Andrew was leader of the pack with the other four fast on his trail. Then right out of the blue, he came to a quick stop without any apparent reason. Roland was immediately behind him

and he yelled an instruction to him. He jumped off his machine and ran away for about forty yards and then looked at his dad who gave him further guidance. The next thing that I saw was him jumping as high as he could into the air and then landing firmly on his heels on top of a small mound in the snow which was hardly noticeable. He repeated this three times and then leant down and just as a magician pulls a rabbit out of a hat, and this was no rabbit, Roland pulled a baby seal out from under the broken snow.

Everyone ran across to him to see the baby seal. It was absolutely beautiful, soft, cuddly, and gorgeous. You could not help but to immediately fall in love with it, as you do with a newborn lamb. Its eyes were adorable and prominent on its head, and it looked so forlorn, soft, and passionate. We passed him around, everyone wanted to hold and hug him, you could not be anything other than affectionate towards him.

There was a real load of chatter and banter going on amongst them and I hadn't a single clue what they were talking about, but it must have been something concerning the seal. Roland took me aside from the group and explained what was happening. Andrew had spotted the dome in the snow and knew instantly that it was the home of a baby seal. How he saw that while he was driving the snowmobile in a snowstorm is unbelievable, but it is just another indication of how good a hunter he is.

When you looked closely, you could see the flat piece of snow which was the baby's nest adjacent to a breath hole used by the mother to come up for air and keep tabs on her offspring. She would call it into the sea to suckle from her nipples after which it would return to the nest. This was covered in snow in the form of a dome which kept it out of the blizzards and snowstorms and acted like its own private little iglu. It also keeps it well hidden from its land predator, the polar bear who loves them to eat. Polar bears do not normally find baby seals by sight. They use their highly developed sense of smell to find their prey. Once found,

they rise onto their hind feet and then lunge forward onto the dome forcing their paws through the dome and catching the baby seal, much in the same way as Roland tried to do, except he was using his feet to break through the dome as he has no power in his hands and arms.

It was now time for me to give the baby seal my last hug as they now wanted to catch the mother who is the grater prize. They firstly tied a rope to the rear flippers and then lowered him into the sea via the breath hole. He would then cry for his mother's attention who would be back to him in seconds. They then gradually hauled in the bait followed by his mother, and when she exited the hole, they would spear her using a harpoon with a rope attached to it. This was the theory, but in practise, it was not as simple. Qamayuq was in charge of handling the baby seal, and Roland was going to spear the mother. He brought the baby back four or five times but was either too quick or maybe too slow and could not entice the mother out of the sea. She would come so far and then stop. The others were watching with some frustration. I felt they thought they could do better themselves. Eventually Andrew took over, but he could not draw her out as she had cottoned onto their plan and she did not want any part of it. I'm sure that if Andrew had been first to lure the mother, then we would have had a mother seal in the bag, but it was not going to happen now.

We had spent enough time trying to catch the mother and we still had a fair ways to go. Andrew told Roland to kill the seal. He then proceeded to spin the seal around in circles and then stopped suddenly with an abrupt jerk which caused its blood to rush into its brain and cause an instant haemorrhage which killed it. Andrew said this was how the polar bears kill them, they would swing them violently from side to side and then suddenly stop. Well, that was another lesson that I had learned about Inuit life and I knew that I would keep learning until the minute that I departed on the plane.

The remaining part of the journey back to Arctic Bay was energetic to say the least. Andrew had his sights set on home and he was going for it. I only hope that he doesn't bust a gut in the process. He had sent his younger son and his friend off to get a welcome party out as they could drive far faster than us because they were not pulling a sledge. I don't know how the others were coping. They all had a lot of stamina and determination, but as sure as eggs are eggs they must be completely whacked by now, I know that I was. When we finally reached the bay itself, there was a remarkable improvement in the weather, but the going was still as bad and I still needed all my agility to stay upright.

We knew that soon we would be within sight of the village and we would be able to rest our weary limbs. I knew exactly what I wanted to do, I was going to have a long hot soak in the bath. While out on the frozen sea, I had never once thought about washing or having a bath. Subconsciously, I knew that it was not possible and the thought never occurred to me. I did not even think of having a shit either. I now know the answer to the question which was also the title of the book that my daughter Jane had bought me.

How do you poo in the Arctic?

Believe me or not, the title is misleading and it is a serious book about surviving in adverse conditions, not just the arctic. The simple answer is that you don't, or you do with great difficulty and at great speed. I honestly only had three 'dumps' in a fortnight and I do not think that the others had any more if even that. I do know that Roland had at least one because he told me and introduced me to their terminology 'dump' when he asked me to stand guard over the breath hole while he went. It must be something to do with your diet and a change in your metabolism. I'll check what happens when I am back in the village and see if things improve.

It seemed that the whole village and their great-grandfathers were awaiting our arrival, and when the snowmobiles came to a stop, everyone let out a big hearty cheer and the kids came running to greet us. Everyone was thrilled that we had succeeded in shooting a polar bear and the kids were pestering Andrew to let them see it, but the answer was a firm, not yet. By now you should be able to guess what his first priority would be. Yes! You're right, it was to release the dogs and tie them down on the chain. Their behaviour had been exemplary. Their effort was inexhaustible, and they had earned a well-deserved celebratory dinner. They must be suffering from cramp and needed to stretch their legs as they had been tightly tied down all the way home. There were several other teams of dogs tied down to the ice and ours knew that they were back home for a while for a well-earned rest. Having rested their vocal chords for quite some time while they were in the kennel on Andrew's sledge, they decided to let rip with the most beautiful chorus which echoed around the bay and stimulated the other teams to partake. It was simply a glorious ensemble of voices from a deep bass to a pitch so high that it has not got a name to describe it. Normally they settle down and stop barking once they all were tied to the chain, but on this occasion, it had become a contest which set the whole bay on fire. It was a delight to watch and to listen to.

We did not leave the ice until the last dog had been fed. Andrew said that he would pick me up in the morning and we would go to the wildlife department and sort out the paperwork, so I picked up my rifle, thanked the team for all their hard work, and walked over to Clare who was waiting to take me back to Kiggavik House.

He opened the conversation by asking me how it went, and then I think he may have wished that he hadn't because now the flood gates were open and I never stopped talking. My enthusiasm kept bubbling out and out and went on continuously until I had to stop to have a celebratory drink. He said that dinner would be in about three hours as we were waiting for the others when they returned from school and they would not be back until school has finished.

'That' is Jim and Jane, is it not?'

'Oh yes, I had forgotten that they were here before you left on tour hunt.'

I wanted to relax in the bath and have a bloody good soak. As I went upstairs, he asked me if I would like another cold beer.

'That's a brilliant idea.'

'I'll bring one up in a minute.'

I remember running to the bath and getting in, but that was all. Clare had brought up my cold beer and left it outside the bedroom door, but I was dead to the wind and never got out of the bath to drink it. It was still there two hours later when he knocked on my door to tell me that dinner would be ready in ten minutes. The bath water had cooled off and I started to shiver when I awoke, so I quickly jumped out and dried myself. Jim and Jane were at the table patiently waiting for me to join them for dinner. I felt a little guilty and certainly embarrassed that the conversation throughout the whole of the dinner totally revolved around my hunt. It was not just my enthusiasm and the fact that I was still bubbling with excitement that focused on the total experience of living on the ice for three weeks with my Inuit friends, but Jim and Jane were genuinely interested, and it was them that were asking all the questions. Eventually, I was able to steer the conversation towards what they were doing in the village and discuss how the Canadian government was helping the Inuits to build into the school curriculum their history, culture, crafts, and skills, so that they are not lost with the pressures exerted by the influence of the white man.

This was what Peter, my carver, was teaching in school and prompted me to apologise for leaving, but I was dying to see if he had finished the carving of the polar bear. His house was only a couple of minutes away, but I still had to put on my outside clothing as I now knew from first-hand experience that it may not look cold but minus thirty is very cold if you are not dressed to combat it.

Peter's wife welcomed me with open arms and pulled me inside. I was about to take off my boots, but she told me not to bother. She said that Peter was at school for a parent–teacher evening, and she did not expect him back for a while. Anna told me that Peter had finished the carving, but it was more than her life was worth to give me a preview. I told her not to worry, and that I had waited three weeks to see it, so an extra day was no trouble. She said that Peter said that I should come around about five the next day for my first carving lesson and have the polar bear unveiled. I thanked her very much and said that I could not wait until the next day to see the carving.

Clare heard me come in and popped out to see if I wanted anything before I went to bed, but I said that Anna had given me a hot chocolate and I was so tired that I could not wait to get into a proper bed for the first time for three weeks. He asked me what time I wanted a call for breakfast, but I asked him if it was if he minded if I had a lie in and woke up naturally without a wake-up call. 'No problem, Dave, I'll cook your breakfast whenever you arise.' I thanked him and said goodnight and climbed the stairs to my room. I was so tired that it was a strain to even undress, but I did and lay my naked body between the cosy linen sheets.

I slept for a solid eleven hours and only woke up because I need a pee. I don't know how long that I would have slept had I not wanted the loo. I had not realised it, but my body certainly had, just how much stress I was under when I was living out on the sea ice for three weeks. The change in diet, the extremely cold temperature, living in constant daylight and not having a fixed routine to awaken and to sleep, all took their toll on my body. It was difficult to appreciate it at the time, as I had to do whatever was necessary to get the job done, but these changes had affected my inner metabolism, even to the extent of not needing to have a 'dump'.

I had a quick shower, which again seemed a privilege, and then went downstairs. Clare was preparing dinner in the kitchen and asked me what I wanted for brunch; breakfast was away long gone. 'I'm not really hungry, Clare, but I could sink a large mug of fresh coffee.'

'No problem, do you want me to bring it to the lounge?'

'No, I'll just have it in here, chat to you, and watch you to prepare dinner.' Clare was making a fish pie, but he was using halibut and not Arctic charr as I had expected him to. By the way Andrew had called around to take you down to the Fish and Game officer, but when I told him you were still in bed, he said that if you looked him up later this afternoon, we could rearrange the appointment.

Although I had an unbelievable time hunting on the sea ice, which I will never forget and would not have swapped the experience for anything else in the world, now that it was over. It was a relief to be back to some kind of normality and the small luxuries which we always take for granted. After I finished my coffee, I decided to go out and explore the village and take some photographs and then call and see Andrew. He promised that he would teach me how to run the dogs and the frozen bay was the perfect. He said that they would not be too fast as they had gorged themselves and these dogs don't run well on a full stomach. I really enjoyed being in control of the dogs, but to be truthfully, they were doing it by themselves as they are so well trained.

The children were on their lunch break and were playing outside. When they saw me, they rushed to the school gate to say hello. These days they are all learning English. I was the white man from Scotland and they all wanted to talk to me, firing question after question. They ignored the school bell to return to class and eventually the teacher had to come out to tell them off. As they ran back to the classroom, the teacher walked across to see me. She said the children were very excited and she asked me if I could come to school the next day for half an hour to chat to the kids. I told her that I would love to do that and asked her what time did she want me.

I continued my walk and took photographs of the churches, the village store, and then I wandered down to the sea to take more photo graphs of the dogs. To see them again was very emotional and brought back those precious memories of my hunt. When Andrew's dogs saw me, I knew that they had recognised me. You can guess what happened next, you're right, my presence started the canine orchestra to start singing and the same happened as it did on our arrival the previous day. Our team stimulated the others to follow suit. There was well over a hundred singing to their hearts' content. The uproar was so loud and intense that some of the villagers came out to see why the dogs were lamenting. When they realised it was me that was causing the uproar, some of them came to see how I was getting on. It was probably because many of the other hunters who have been to Arctic Bay to hunt immediately go home and show little interest in the Inuits or their village, but to me this Arctic experience was more than just killing a polar bear. I wanted to learn how having their own territory after years of not being recognised has changed their lives.

When I called to see Andrew, it was his turn to be out, so after being in each other's pocket for three weeks, we now were having difficulty finding each other. Another of his sons invited me in for a coffee, and I was introduced to the rest of his family and met his daughter and granddaughter. She was really cute and it did not take long to have some fun. We played hide and seek and then I asked her to come and give me a cuddle. Much to her mother's surprise, she ran across the room and jumped into the arms of a stranger. I was pleased as Punch; I really had been accepted into the hearts of the Inuits and was lapping up all the affection. While I was there, Roland arrived, he said that he had really had loved hunting with me and showed me the pictures he had taken. There were some really good photographs, and he had the snap of all four of us around the polar bear. He promised that he would burn me a copy and I could collect it in the morning when I came back to see his dad. Before I left, he asked me if I would like to come and watch him play ice hockey tomorrow evening at half seven.

'Where's the hockey pitch?' half-expecting it to be somewhere on the sea ice or in the school yard, but he said it was in the stadium. 'We take our ice hockey very seriously.' He went on to tell me that there is great rivalry in the village. I suppose that it's like Celtic and Rangers in Scotland, but I never expected them to have a stadium. However, on reflection, I suppose that in the months of total darkness, a stadium will be a big asset to the village and keep the community together.

When I got back to Kiggavik House, I decided to look at my photographs, a ten-gig card holds over five thousand pictures in high definition, and I had taken over three thousand. Sometimes I took over ten pictures to make sure that I got a good one. Since digital cameras were introduced onto the market, I like millions of others have had a renewed interest in photography and taken it more seriously. What only the professional photographers could do in the past is now within the grasp of anyone with a serious interest in photography I have already sold some photographs through an agency which creates even more enthusiasm to improve. I sat in the lounge looking at the photographs and removing the rubbish which were out of focus or a poor picture. When I'm unsure about a photograph, I leave it so that I can see it on the laptop at a much-increased size and improved definition. I was relaxing in the lounge with a cold beer editing my photographs and admiring the good ones when suddenly the LCD screen went blank. I went frantic. I was unable to get a single photograph. I was delirious pressing button after button, but I still could not see a picture. I yelled out, 'Oh shit, fuck, fucking hell, what the hell have I done.' Clare rushed in from the kitchen to see what was happening. I was sitting with my head in my hands virtually crying. 'What's wrong, Dave?'

'I've wiped off all the photographs on my camera. I've ruined the opportunity of writing a book to help the Inuits of Arctic Bay and the polar bears. Without any pictures, my book will be useless. Oh, what the fuck have I done!'

Clare tried to calm me down and then said it might not be the end of the day and we might be able to get them back.

'Oh Christ, Clare, they're gone! How can we get them back?' Clare was trying to explain what I would have to do when I got home, when Jim walked in. He could see that I was extremely upset, and Clare told him what I had done. 'Don't worry, Dave, I'm sure that I can fix it. Let me take my bag upstairs and I'll have a go.' I had arranged to go and see Peter to collect my polar bear and have my first stone carving lesson, so I left my camera with Jim and went across the road to Peter's house.

Peter was back from school and waiting outside for me, ready to start my first lesson. He had the small carvings that that he had made for my grandchildren with him, but he was going to keep me waiting to see the polar bear carving which was in the house. The little carvings for the kids were great. There was a whale, a seal, a walrus and he had made a bunny rabbit for little Eive. He then looked around on his pile of rocks and picked up a piece little bigger than a tennis ball and started to rough it out using a disc saw with a stone cutting blade. He had me shitting bricks. I was so nervous watching him as he brought the blade which was rotating at over three thousand revolutions a minute within millimetres of his fingers. I stood there, mouth open, gasping for air, and not daring to move a muscle in case I distracted him and caused an accident. Within a couple of minutes, he had it roughed it out and I was able to identify the animal which he was carving. He had a natural and remarkable gift and was able to turn a rough piece of stone into a carving of an animal with a few strokes of a disk saw. Thankfully he switched off the angle grinder which was a gigantic relief to me and then he passed it to me to examine and said, 'There you are, you can finish it off, Dave'.

'Not with the angle grinder I hope.'

'No, you can finish it with a grinding wheel on a cable drill.' I didn't know where to start, so he took back the carving and the drill and showed me exactly what to do. We were trying to carve a whale with its tail held high into the air. I was doing quite well but held the wheel onto it for a fraction of a second too long and whipped of the tail before I could correct myself. Peter told me not to worry and picked up another rock and started again. He was back using the disk grinder again sapping away all of my nervous energy just watching him. It was back to me again, but this time I was even more careful to avoid ruining my carving, and Peter was pleased with my performance. I started to struggle as I was approaching the tail, so he decided to help and give another demonstration of how I should use the grinding wheel. I could not believe my eyes when the old master accidentally cut off a fin. 'See, Dave, it can happen to the best of us. I have had some very delicate and intricate carvings which have taken me hours and within minutes of completion ruined by one careless move.' I looked at him with despair and then we started again on the third carving. This time we managed to achieve a nice carving which I am proud to say looks very good.

'Are you going to show me the polar bear now, Peter? I am dying to see it.' My patience was starting to be exhausted. I had been back in the village for twenty-four hours, and I still had not had the unveiling of my commission. 'No, I wanted to do one more thing.' He leant forwards and picked up another piece of rock, followed by his disc saw and started to rough out yet another animal. His skill is frankly awesome. He must have studied the animals of the Arctic for hours to be able to carve the way he does. He passed me the rock and said that I had to take this home and finish the walrus which he had made and bring the finished carving when I returned to Arctic Bay for his approval. He even gave me a piece of caribou antler to make the walruses tusks with. 'Right, let's go inside and I'll show you the polar bear.'

We dusted down our clothes to avoid taking the stone dust into the house and then took them off inside the porch. Anna welcomed me inside and bid me to take a seat next to a small table upon which there was something covered over with a towel, which I envisaged was the polar bear. Peter stepped across to unveil it, and I was ecstatic. It was simply an unbelievable piece of art and was carved in exactly the position that I had requested. The bear was leaning forwards with its arms outstretched ready to pounce on a baby seal which was hidden just under the ice. He had carved the baby seals as well and I was more than happy with the result which I'm sure you'll agree is a masterpiece and warrants a prime position in my collection when I get it home.

As we sat and had a coffee while I was still admiring the polar bear, Anna asked me if I would like to stay for dinner as she had cooked a typical Inuit dish. I said, 'Clare is expecting me back to eat.' But she said that he would not mind and offered me the phone to ring him. I felt very embarrassed as I knew that he had prepared the meal but did not want to offend her either, so I asked her if she would ring him. She said, 'No problem', and she took the phone from me and proceeded to ring him. The answer was just as she had said it would be, so she started to put it out. As soon as she lifted the lid of the casserole dish, the aroma hit you instantly. It was a rich meaty smell and very enticing and I could see it bubbling away in a thick brown gravy.

'What have you cooked for me, Anna?' But before she could even utter a word, Peter interrupted and said I should try it first and then have a guess. He really is a bugger for keeping a secret. We all sat down at the table and I attempted to put a spoonful into my mouth, but it was so bloody hot that it burnt my tongue, but there was just sufficient to absorb the flavour. It was simply delicious, a little beefy but had its own subtle flavour. It was obvious that it was not caribou, but I shudder to think what it was and I didn't manage to guess. 'I give up, what is it, Peter?' He looked quite astonished as he had expected me to guess, and when he told me that it was musk ox, I knew that I should have known as the are not many land animals in the Arctic to choose from. Now that the puzzle was over, we set to give it a good home and there was not a drop of gravy left on any of our plates. It was another first for me and a very enjoyable one too.

Peter said that he would like to drive me to the airport when I left and he said that he would pack up all the carvings so that they would not get broken, and I promised to keep them in my hand luggage and not let them out of my sight. I thanked both of them very much and bid them goodnight. Then I walked across the road to bed. I was wondering how Jim had got on with my camera and I expected that I would have to wait until the morning to find out, but much to my surprise, both Jim and Clare were still chatting in the lounge. Clare asked me if I had enjoyed my dinner with Peter and Anna, and I told him what Anna had cooked and that it was delicious.

Jim asked me if I wanted the good news or the bad news first. I said, 'Tell me the good news.'

'I can fix it and get your pictures back, but I need a special link lead to go from my laptop to your camera and I have not got one with me, but I will write down what you have to do and someone in Scotland can mend it.'

On hearing that Clare interrupted, 'No, we need to fix it here so that Dave can relax. I think that I've got one in my office, hold on a minute.' He walked swiftly into his office and returned with a glum face but said that he is sure that one of the teachers have got one and he gave her a ring. 'You're in luck, Dave, I'll just nip out and get it.'

'There's no rush, Clare, the morning will do.' But by this time he was putting his coat on and on the way.

Jim decided to stay up and wait for Clare as it would only take a few minutes to reinstall the photographs once he has the lead. I could not tell him how grateful I was as I hadn't the words to explain, and when I told him why and my motives for writing the book, he said that if he could not fix it here in Arctic Bay, he would take memory card home and then post it to me in Scotland. We did not have to wait long. Clare was soon back with a grin like a Cheshire cat, as he was dangling the lead in his hand. 'I've got it. Let's give it a twirl.' He passed the lead to Jim who took it into the dining room and connected it to his computer. 'Voilà! I've cracked it,' were the words which echoed around the dining room and brought elation into the lounge. Clare and I immediately rushed to see for ourselves. 'It's true Clare, Jim has recovered them all.' I've never felt so relived in my life and gave Jim a big hug and a thank you. 'I'm so pleased that I could help such a good cause.' He was of course referring to the book. Clare was pleased as well and went into the kitchen to get a celebratory drink and returned with three large mugs of hot chocolate which went down a treat before we went to bed.

I awoke early the next morning. This was my last day in Arctic Bay and I had a very busy schedule, my first port of call was to meet Andrew at his house as we had an appointment with the Fish and Game officer. I knocked on his door several times, but there was no reply, so I sat on his snowmobile and watched the dogs on the ice while I waited for Andrew to wake. I was patiently waiting when

there was a knock on the widow. Andrew was waving and then opened the door and told me to come in.

Once he was dressed, we had breakfast together and then headed for the Fish and Game office. The officer had already heard that I had killed a bear and that we had to shoot another because of the problem with the dogs. As is usually the case, there was a lot of government paperwork to be completed and he had to take measurements and remove two teeth from the skull. The skull from my bear was going to be boiled and bleached and I asked him what he was going to do with the skull off the female which we killed. He did not want it and said that I could have it if I wanted. I didn't want it all as I would have difficulty getting it through customs, so he offered to cut off a short muzzle which would contain the upper and lower incisors and took it into the workshop. He was back in a matter of minutes and passed it to me. It just needed a gentle boiling which Clare did for me.

Andrew and I wandered back to his house and brewed another coffee. After we drank it, Andrew had to get ready as he was flying to Qikiqtarjuaq for a meeting and I had to call into the school for a chat with the kids. But first I had to call in and see Qamayuq and thank him for all he had done and give him a big tip. I knew

that it was going to be difficult to communicate as he did not speak a word of English. I knocked on the door and then suddenly remembered that it was not etiquette to knock. The door was answered by a very good-looking young lady. 'You must be Dave.' 'Yeh,' I nodded my head, and she invited me in, and I sighed with relief as I now would be able to talk to Qamayuq. Nina was his daughter and was on vacation from university for a few weeks. Qamayuq was very proud of her and rightly so, from the small quiet school in Arctic Bay she had graduated with a first-class honours in law at the university in Ottawa. I asked her to tell him that I have had without doubt the most fantastic three weeks of my life. We reminisced for a while on our hunt miles out on the sea ice, where day after day we searched in vain for the polar bear. We never gave up on the hunt and it took to the very last day to find our bear. It was now time to go to the school as I knew the kids would be waiting for me. I thanked him once more, and he told me that I was now a true friend of the Inuits in Arctic Bay and that I had to come back again to hunt with them. Just as I was walking out of the door, he shouted of me to stop and he rushed to his freezer and took out two Arctic charr and a block of seal meat for me to take back to Scotland. It was very generous of him, but I did not know how the hell was I going to take that back home. I thanked him and headed off for the school.

It was a really nice session. The children were very excited and there was no shortage of questions, and where they could not ask me in English, the teacher helped out. Most of the questions were about Scotland or Great Britain, but some were about where else I had hunted in the world. I reckon that I could have been there for the rest of the day, but they had to get their lunch and so had I.

I spent some of the afternoon sitting on the porch writing up my notes, but I had to keep going inside to thaw out and it was very difficult writing with gloves on. You know it really is uncanny, you have a beautiful clear blue sky and pristine white snow and you don't realise that it is minus thirty until you remove your gloves, when the frost bites fiercely into your fingers. Eventually I gave up trying to write outside and went into the lounge to finish it off. Clare called us in for dinner. As this was my last night in Arctic Bay, Clare had roasted a saddle of caribou with wild mushrooms, lava seaweed, and potatoes. The meat was cooked medium rare and was so succulent that it melted in your mouth and took little chewing.

I had one more appointment this evening and as I did not want to be late, I left my sweet until I returned after the match. Roland was playing ice hockey this evening and he wanted me to come and watch. I put on my Arctic clothing and then walked down to the ice rink which was only ten minutes away. The match had already started and it took a good ten minutes to work out which one was Roland as they are all in the same kit and have a protective helmet which covers their faces. Actually the truth of the matter was that Roland saw me and came to the edge of the rink to say hello rather than me spotting him. From then on, I was able to pick him out as he was wearing number eleven. As I was watching

the match, an elderly gentleman came up to me for a chat, and much to my surprise, he was able to talk in English. He had worked in Ottawa for several years and his English was pretty good. I asked him about some of the rules which I did not understand and how long the game lasts. He told me that they play for three hours, a hour and a half each way. 'By god, they must be exhausted after that. I'm sure that our matches in the UK don't last that long.' There weren't many spectators, but the few that were there nearly raised the roof when our side scored a goal. The rivalry between the two sides is very strong and they do take the game seriously. I suppose that with not much else to do, they throw themselves wholeheartedly into the matches. The comradely is great fun both on and off the ice and the game is played by men and women alike, and if they are short of numbers, there is often a mixed team. I asked him if he used to play ice hockey and he said that he still does.

'We have a pensioner's match once a week.'

'And how long do you play for?' I expected him to say half an hour or so.

'We play for three hours as well just the same as them.' He pointed to the players on the ice.

'How old are you then?'

'Oh, I'm seventy-two.' I must admit that I was astounded and wondered if he was filling me with a load of bullshit.

There was no break at half time. They just changed ends, but I managed to grab a word with Roland to say a final goodbye, but he said that he would come up to Clare's place to say a final adios in the morning and then he immediately rejoined the game. I turned to say goodbye to the old man and thanked him for explaining the rules to me. He asked me to return again next year and watch him play. If I did return, then I would find out if the pensioners had the strength and endurance to last for three hours. 'Good God, I'm nearly a pensioner and I could not last even one hour. These Inuits don't have a lot of guts.'

Clare had kept my sweet warm in the oven, but it had passed its best as it had fallen with keeping. Soufflés should be eaten straight out of the oven. It may have lost a bit of its texture but certainly it hadn't lost any of its flavour. The Arctic wild berries were so good that I went back for seconds.

I reflected on my time in the Arctic which was now drawing to a close. In the morning, I would have to catch my plane back to Ottawa. There is no doubt that this unexpected hunt and expedition in the Arctic had been an unbelievable success and mind-blowing experience. To me hunting is not focused on killing, I can unequivocally say that it mattered not to me whether or not I squeezed the trigger, I had enjoyed and learned so much about life in the Arctic and in particular, my Inuit hosts who were truly excellent and for three weeks we had shared our lives together, the finality of killing the polar bear was an insignificant part of the whole deal. This hunt was unlike any others where the 'professional

hunters' were trained to hunt and track animals. I was undoubtedly with a natural hunter, a man whose mere survival and that of his family is dependent on his hunting skills which have been passed down from generation to generation. I was grateful that I had the opportunity of living with true aboriginal hunters and partaking in their lifestyle.

When I returned to Ottawa, Joe was there to greet me. He already knew that I had shot my polar bear and he had another satisfied client to add to the endless list of hunters.

I knew then that I could expect a remarkable moose hunt in the fall. Joe drove me back to his house to stay for the night before I crossed the pond in the morning.

While we were waiting at the airport, Joe was quizzing me when my next hunt would be and what I wanted to hunt. I had not quite made up my mind, but I still wanted a whitetail and an elk, but I would not go to any other agent or outfitters when you know you have the best and there's no one in their right mind would want to move. He strives to be the best. He only uses the best outfitters and in my opinion, I would never go past Natura Sports He is not the cheapest, but you will never be disappointed with any hunt Joe has to offer, try him: jo. verni@videotron. ca. I now have been hunting for over fifty years and have really enjoyed my hunting and shooting and at the same time I have always had a deep interest in nature and the environment, which started when I was four of five when I would spend hours watching birds, mice, and rabbits. When I grew older, I spent hour upon hour watching and photographing animals and birds and enjoyed every moment. I have no regrets about hunting as all the animals that I have killed have been killed for food including the polar bear, which is still and in the future will be hunted by the Inuits for food. You have got to remember that polar bears, seals, and whales are as much part of their diet as chickens, lambs, and cows are of ours.

Now, I would let you have an insight into the other side of my life, one which I have enjoyed since childhood and one that I will be perusing and enjoying in the future. I am still going to hunt and even more vigorously, but on all occasions in the future I will be armed only with a camera or two or three, and will be dedicating my time to promoting this book and the conservation of the polar bear and helping the Inuit people in the Arctic

You may be jealous and think that I have been lucky. Well, in part you right, I have been lucky in what I have witnessed in many parts of the world and this had not been limited to wildlife .I have had the privilege and the opportunity to visit far-reaching countries and that is why I am not going to stop now. I believe that you can make your own luck by who you are and the messages that you send out to your fellow man, no matter what colour, religion and whether they are rich or poor. These vibes they receive from you sets the foundations of how your relationship will develop as it does with all communications in any part of life, including the animal kingdom. If an animal or bird thinks that it is safe in your presence and not a threat, then it will relax, show itself at its best and sometimes let you into its inner secrets. I hope you enjoy some of the magical moments that I have appreciated and love over my last fifty years.

I initially wrote the book entitled "The Arctic, The Inuit and Polar Bear. A Half century of Hunting", which I have already written, however the publishers suggested that it was too long and that I should split it into two books. The benefit of that is that we should sell more books and raise more money for the Inuit Village of Arctic Bay and also to protect the Polar Bears as best we can.

Now that I have changed from a hunter to a photographer, this is a sample of the photographs that will be included in my next book along with the stories that made them possible.

TALES FROM A HALF CENTURY OF HUNTING

How Did I Get This Passion for Hunting, Where Did It Come From?

My father was a farmer's son, hand reared on a small farm of only eighty acres called Angerton in the village of Kirkbride in Cumbria. In those days, a small farm like Angerton could keep two generations in work. He worked there until he was twenty-five when his father was ill. He was the only son out of seven children, and unlike the norm, where the eldest boy follows on and keeps farming, the farm was sold. He had to find a new job and five generations of the Hills farming Angerton was broken.

My first five years were closely associated with the farm and the seeds of farming had been sown and germinated and it was my lifetime's ambition to be a farmer and mend the broken link. I can remember when Dad used to go into the byre to milk the cows by hand and I would stand there, mouth open waiting for him to divert the milk to me. He was a very good shot and always managed to hit my face if not my mouth. My passion for hunting arose in those early days too, when Dad used to take me shooting rabbits which could damage a crop of carrots or oats beyond repair and ruin the crop. At other times of the year, he used a ferret to bolt them into a net, and then he would dispatch them with a 'rabbit punch' which was a blow to the back of the head.

After the farm was sold, I used to spend some weekends and holidays at Oulton House which was where my uncle farmed. He loved shooting, and on the first day of September, the opening day of the shooting season, I used to go with Uncle John and be by his side when he was shooting duck and partridge. Auntie Annie, my dad's sister, used to cook them to perfection and introduced me to the taste of game, which I have enjoyed throughout my life. I used to play with my cousin Keith and we were always into trouble. I remember that we were caught on one occasion using Uncle John's air rifle and taking potshots at one of their many cats. The other memory that was always vivid in my memory and still is was watching Uncle Jack. He wasn't really anyone's uncle but a long and endearing friend who was in his late seventies. On the first of May every year, he used to go with his 22 rifle to shoot 'squarkers'. These are fledging rooks that were just about to fly and sat cautiously on the edge of the nest or in the branches, plucking up courage to have their maiden flight. I can close my eyes and remember him cycling into the cobbled farmyard with two bundles of young rooks hanging from the handlebars and his rifle swung around his back. He used to call me little Davy, and I could stay for hours listening to his stories while he puffed away on his pipe which he filled with 'black twist', a very strong tobacco which he cut off and then rolled it in his hands to soften it before he used it to fill his pipe. Nana, my gran, always made rook pie or should I say pies, in the first weeks of May. That is probably where the nursery rhyme stems from.

> Four and twenty black birds,
> Baked in a pie,
> When the pie was opened,
> The birds began to sing,
> Wasn't that a dainty dish,
> To put before the King.

I used to spend the vast majority of my weekends and school holidays with Moo and Pop, my mother's parents. They had a small holding and reared pigs for bacon. This period of my life was instrumental in the development of my love of food, cooking, and hunting. Moo etched out my basic philosophy of life and used to say and I quote, 'It's better to know a little about everything rather a lot about naught', unquote and that is still how I think today. She introduced me to cooking and started my interest in travelling. As a little boy, I used to tell her that I would be off around the world now, but I'll be back for lunch. To this day, I love and will always love travelling and learning about how all the different people live their lives and what is important to them.

I will never forget 20 April 1959. Sewells who farmed the next farm to Moo were retiring and having a farm sale. I was there early in the morning to view the lots and noticed that lot sixty-one was a four ten shotgun with two boxes of cartridges. This was nicknamed the poacher's gun as it folded in two and you could stick it under your coat. I could not get it out of my mind and went to the sale in the afternoon hoping to buy it. I sat for what seemed hours waiting for lot sixty-one to be sold, hoping that I had enough money to purchase it. The minutes were slowly ticking away until at last I heard that lot fifty-nine was a set of hames, which are part of the livery, that you use when you are getting a cart horse ready to go into the field and work. It was well sort after and the bidding seemed to be endless. Lot sixty was a set of hand tools, sickles and scythes. I listened to the auctioneer take the bids.

'I'm asking two pounds here. Who's going to open the bidding? This is a handy lot, five tools. Come on, now.'

'One pound and half a crown.'
'Come on there.'
'I'll take one pound.'
'I have got one pound and six pence.'
'Do I have a bid there?'
'One pound and twenty pence.'
'Now I have got one pound and nine shillings.'
'Can I ask two pounds?'

'All right, I'll take one pound and nine shillings. I'm selling it. One pound and nine shillings once. One pound and ten shillings twice. Last chance, it' going.'

Then he hit his hammer on the bench, gone. The next lot would be my four ten shotgun. I was very, very nervous. Did I have the courage to stand there and bid against all of these farmers? Was I big enough to be noticed? My head was spinning out of control. I had never been to a farm auction before and did not really know the ins and outs and how to bid. Should I raise my hand like I had to do at school to ask the teacher a question? Should I wink at the auctioneer as I saw some farmers doing or should I shout at him? There were pimples all over my arms, and I felt myself blushing with nerves. One, two, three, and it was to be lot sixty-one. I waited anxiously, telling myself that I could do it.

Now it was my turn, the unfolding of my hunting life, and it never happened, the auctioneer boldly said, 'We are moving on to lot sixty-two as lot sixty-one has been withdrawn'. It floored me. I was astounded. My heart sunk. I had waited all this time and told myself that I would bid and would not chicken out at the last minute. Then after all those expectation and dreams of me shooting rabbits and crows, it was no longer there. What had happened? Why was the gun withdrawn? How would I find out where it was?

I had lost all interest in the auction and walked away from the sale ring, deflated and upset. I decided to go to the farmhouse to see John Sewell and find out from the horse's mouth exactly what had happened. Mrs Sewell answered the door, 'What can I do for you, lile Davey?'

'Is Mr Sewell in?'

'Aye, he's in the snug having a few puffs.' He was sitting on his favourite rocking chair with old Tom curled up in his lap. He was next to the aga puffing away on his briar pipe, 'Is-t thou gay thrang, what's dangled thee laddie, thou looks as though the bottom has dropped out of the sky'? 'Well, I've stood all afternoon watching the auction as I wanted to buy your old four ten and when it got to lot sixty-one, it had been withdrawn and I had set my heart on getting that gun, so I could shoot Moo's rabbits.'

'That's what's bothering thee then. Well, James the auctioneer told me that it was illegal to sell it at an auction and I had no choice but to withdraw it. Anyway, thee could not have bought it in any case thou is too young.'

'Oh please, sell it to me, Mr Sewell, I really wanted that gun, and Moo said that it was all right if I shot her rabbits.'

His answer was a straight no. I was too young and he was not going to get in a tiff with the law so that was the end of the matter. 'Here, have a glass of Jersey milk, that will set thou right.' 'I don't want a glass of milk. I want to buy your gun.' I pleaded with him, and he was not going to change his mind until Mrs Sewell intervened saying, 'You don't have to sell him the gun but you could give it to him. We've known wee Davy since he came out of nappies and he is a good boy and never been in any trouble.'

Mr Sewell thought long and hard and then said, 'OK, I'll give thou it but on one condition, before you have it, you have to come here and I'll come with thee and make sure your safe before you have it.' I was jumping up and down with excitement like any ten-year-old that had found a three-penny piece. 'Oh, thank you, thank you, Mr Sewell. You will not regret this. I will come and shoot all your rabbits for you. Wait till I go and tell Moo. She'll be damned thrilled that I can get rid of those pests for her.'

My heart nearly exploded with excitement when I told Moo. She said that I could not mess around with it as it was dangerous but was much happier when I told her that Mr Sewell was going to set me right before he gave it to me. This may not sound a big deal to my American hunting friends, where you can have a gun soon after you can walk, but to us it is very much a big deal, you can't have a gun until your are gone eighteen.

Mr Sewell had given me two boxes of cartridges and I was set and ready to go. The first morning I went hunting was on my tenth birthday, 24 April 1959, and I shot my first rabbit at eleven thirty. Fifty years later, a full half-century, that's two thousand and nine I was in the Arctic hunting for a polar bear.

I shot at some rabbits that were running, bang! Bang! I had missed them with both barrels. I tried to shoot some pigeons and some more rabbits and had blown a full box of cartridges by lunchtime when I went home with only one rabbit. Something had to change and change fast as once the second box was finished, I did not have enough pocket money to buy any more. I must shoot enough rabbits or pigeons to sell so that I could buy my next box of cartridges.

That is when I stopped shooting and started stalking. This was also the start of a bad habit as far as shotgun shooting was concerned. I got into the habit of poking and not swinging, but from then on I always had some money in the kitty to buy my next box of cartridges. I always took my game to 'Fishers' in Carlisle. They were fishmongers and game dealers, and he always gave me a good price. They were still there forty years later, but the owners have passed away and that part of Carlisle has been redeveloped and the supermarkets have moved in.

I became a very good stalker and would crawl along a stane dyke and surprise my quarry. I managed to stalk hares, pheasants, partridge, and on one occasion,

I even shot a fox. As time passed by and money was not too much of a problem, I did start to shoot moving game, anything going away from me was as good as dead, but if they went sideways, they had a good chance of surviving.

When I eventually traded in my four ten for a twelve gauge, the gunsmith looked down the barrel and asked me if I had been shooting with it. I told him that I had shot a lot of rabbits and he told me that I was bloody lucky to be here. It was a ticking time bomb awaiting to explode, the barrel was so pitted. That was my first lesson in gun care and now all my weapons are in an immaculate condition.

Hunting became a major part of my life. When I turned eighteen, I applied for my first fire arms licence and shot gun certificate. I bought a Rugar .22 and a Tikka .222. This was the real start of my hunting career, I have shot a lot of foxes and roe deer with the .222 rifle, too many to remember. The rest is in the books. It is perfect for hunting on my farm where the shots are anywhere from fifty to a hundred and fifty yards because of the mixture of the woods, the terrain, and the fields.